Heavenly Demonic

MORTAL REALM

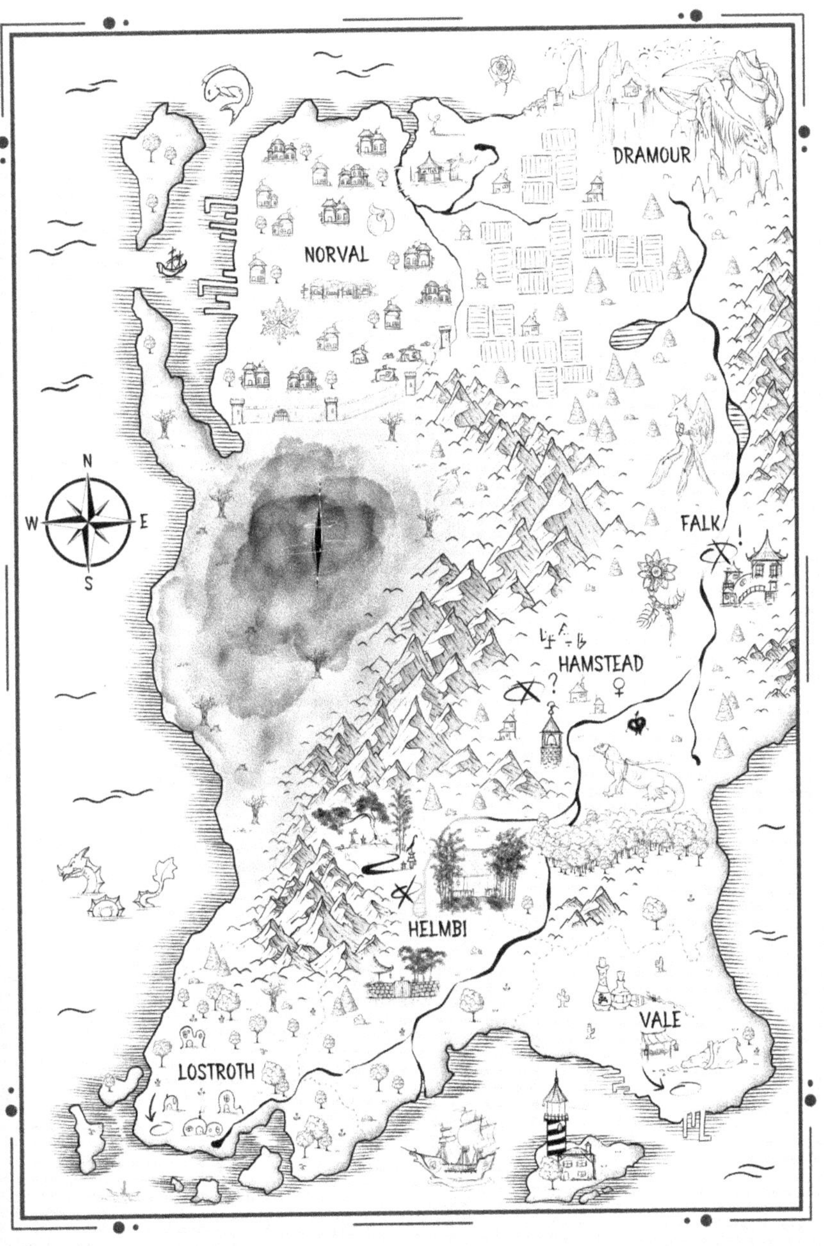

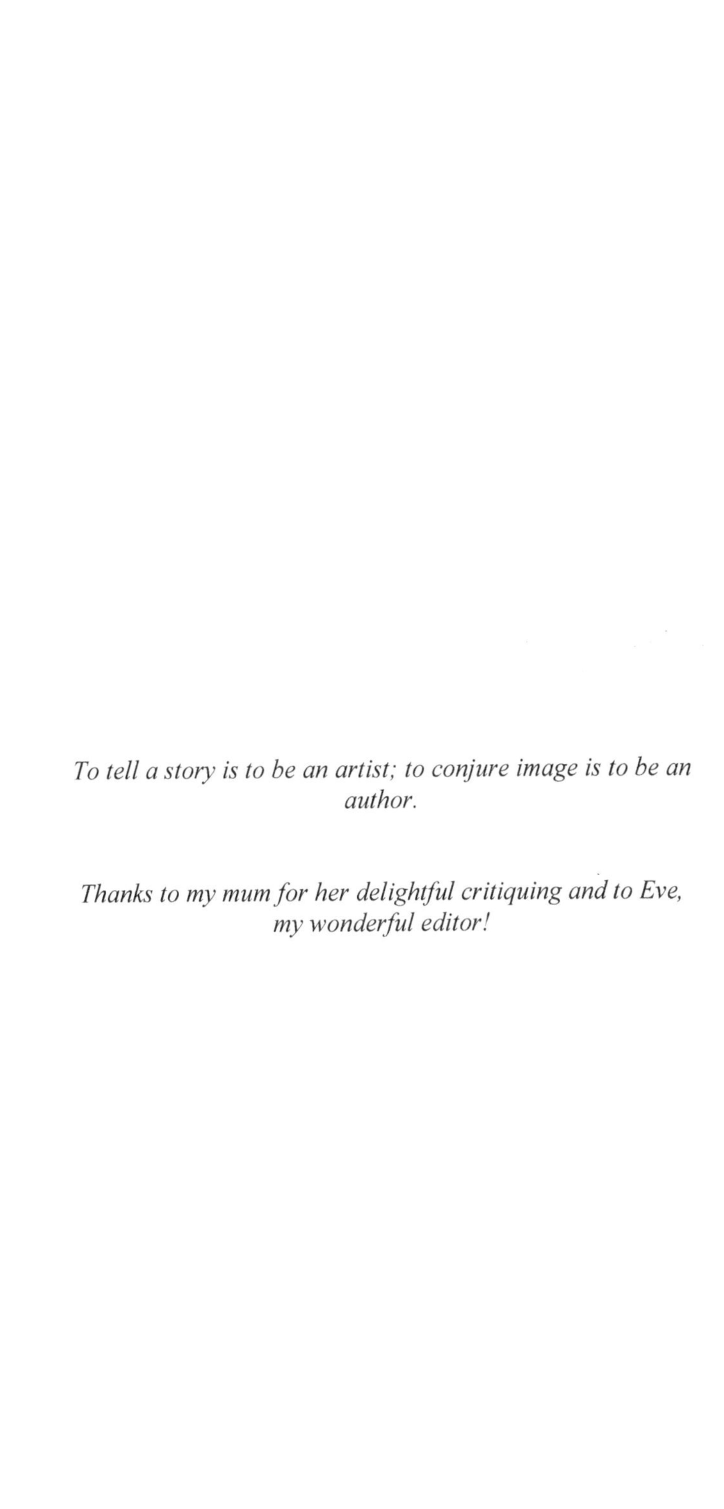

To tell a story is to be an artist; to conjure image is to be an author.

Thanks to my mum for her delightful critiquing and to Eve, my wonderful editor!

Prologue

The bitterness of lazy winter had thrown its first tantrum as autumn swiftly departed with the last hope of warmth. The ground was lightly covered with freshly fallen snow. Trees that stood bare at the town's edge held clusters of huddling birds, who forwent migrating in defiance of the harsh winds and faced the days to come with bold tenacity.

The same went for the people who lived here in Dramour. Built around, through, and on multiple mountainsides with cliffs so sheer that stomachs churned and waterfalls so tall they rivalled the majestic dragon's great length, the eternal flowering city proudly perched.

Within this interconnected kingdom, spirits were at an all-time high. It mattered not that the weather disagreed, as the most grandiose festival had seized the land. The Festival of Celestial Arts brought people together from far and wide.

It was a time when anyone and everyone could show their worth to the gods through the arts. If the emperor of the heavenly realm considered your talent exceptional, you were guaranteed to ascend and take your station amongst the worthy. If not, the cloaked heavenly immortals roaming the city, enjoying what the festival had to offer, would also keep an eye out for potential understudies. Haise Alsta had been to the festival only once before and was too young to remember the experience. His family had struggled for many years but had always made sure to save for the festival, so he'd promised them he would enjoy it and make it as memorable as possible.

Throughout the city, he could spot all manner of sculptures boasting incredible craftsmanship. Most bore a resemblance to a worshipped deity. Those that took the shape of leaping animals and tiny spirits appeared to struggle against their frozen forms, willing their small sculpted bodies to bounce and their wings to flutter. Among the festival lights, dance and song brought old tales of love and valour to life. In tiered dresses, performers leapt side to side on the cobbled streets. Ribbons of bright cloth followed their path, twirling obediently to a rhythm only they shared.

Told in layers of paint, stories of great calamities that had shaken the realms took hold of canvases and strangled out their light. Haise took in the swirls of white-painted silk that flowed from the waist of a forlorn maiden. He preferred this scene to the more lurid canvases that screamed out for attention.

Shoving past him, children ran and played with intricate playthings. Unperturbed by the sudden jostle, Haise watched as their toys came to life when thrown to the heavens, each one gliding on handcrafted wings or similar appendages.

The smell of food hung in the air, the choices varying from the traditionally festive to the wild spices of Vale that took your tongue to foreign lands. Haise acknowledged the impossibility of tasting everything and decided instead to be thankful he was there amid the flamboyant crowds of artisans.

Heavenly music continued to flow on the wind as hushed voices awaited the arrival of the head of the Immortal Clan, patriarch of the leading family branch, the House of Eternal Blossoms: Zander Emrys, who was to arrive with his only heir, Yasu Emrys. Yasu would take on the patriarch role after his father's passing, and he happened to be Haise's age, though Haise often wondered why everyone placed him on a pedestal. Catching a glimpse of him was rare; most hadn't even seen a painting of his image. Yasu, the little heir, seemed distant and so fragile that a slight breeze could crumble him into dust. Haise had seen this from time to time when he snuck into the Immortal Clan's estate. It was as if Yasu's body were present but his heart and soul were somewhere else.

Now I take the risk for joy . . .

Haise had always thought it strange that Yasu's life was so strict. Understanding and fulfilling his duties was one thing, but being unable to attend the festival afterwards was another. To Haise, it seemed like utter nonsense. The patriarch thought too highly of his family, so high he dared not allow his son to prattle with the commoners. Haise decided he'd rather not stick around to hear the ingenuine speech to come, knowing full well it was nothing Yasu wished to say, so he left to buy a gift for his mother. Although he had little money, it would at least be one birthday he hadn't missed.

That evening, long after the speeches were told and the present was bought, he stumbled into the fickle hands of fate when he came upon Yasu standing between two marquees, humming a gentle melody that they had created together. Startled by Haise's sudden appearance, the fireflies that had come to rest on Yasu's shoulders began flitting about, twinkling in frustration.

I pray the keeper miss my ploy . . .

Yasu took a nervous step away; the dazzling festival lights behind Haise cast a long shadow. The cold winds caused Haise's cheeks to blush, and he quickly said, "Wait! It's me, Haise."

Now that Haise was close enough to see Yasu's face, it made him feel out of place, for what he saw was no longer boyish charm. Yasu's attire for the festival was the definition of elegance and refinement, except for his hair, which had been bundled in the same state of dishevelment Haise had always seen it in.

Haise giggled; the look was certainly unique. Yasu didn't seem to mind, as he smiled, laughing a little as well.

"Let me fix your hair." Haise beckoned him closer.

Peering down towards Haise's hand, Yasu saw a small wooden crane. Painted all white and adorned with a circlet, the crane stood regal despite its humble origins. It was the gift Haise had meant for his mother. He had grabbed it earlier from a toy stall nearby.

He knew his mother would be more upset that he hadn't purchased food instead, so with much deliberation and a slight frown, Haise stretched out his hand and delivered it carefully to the heir.

"Are . . . are you giving this to me?" The unexpected gift took Yasu aback. Apart from Haise, no one willingly approached him because of his father, so gifts and friends were almost nonexistent. Haise wasn't scared of Yasu's father or his dogs or his status as patriarch.

Smiling gently, Haise coughed under his breath. "Of course. My mother would scold me if I brought it home. She would have wanted me to spend my coin on food."

Yasu gratefully took the wooden crane and sat, delighted, while Haise retied his hair.

If death shows before day's end . . .

"I promise to cherish it for all eternity," he said with a firm resolve that surprised Haise. He realised that no one but Yasu ever took anything he said or did seriously.

"A thanks would do, Your Heir-y-ness." Haise teasingly bowed while pulling out the bottom of his shirt in an attempt to curtsy. Yasu laughed, and Haise grabbed his hand, guiding them onto the street.

Haise had thought he already knew quite a bit about Yasu, but meandering through the crowds and shops, he learnt much more. Yasu had a weakness for sweet food, could make anything out of paper, and had read almost every book within the Immortal Clan's library, including the secret room, to which members of the House of Eternal Blossoms had exclusive access.

He even told Haise that he hated his last name and thanked him for always calling him Yasu. Haise knew better than to pry but it didn't stop his curiosity; it only suppressed its vocalisation.

As the festival drew to an end, Yasu appeared to grow more anxious. Haise watched him as he glanced around, his eyes wandering over everything. Based on Yasu's fixed stares at whatever he picked up, it was easy to deduce that repayment was on his mind, even though Haise neither had asked nor wished for anything in return.

Haise was about to tell Yasu not to worry, as he knew firsthand how tricky it could be to pick out a present for someone, but Yasu looked determined. Yet he seemed to be finding the exercise particularly difficult, as every item he picked up went straight back down. Haise didn't want to hurt his feelings by rejecting his effort; still, there was no such thing as a perfect gift.

He paused next to a stall, his thoughts shifting to the contents. On display were various feminine trinkets, such as jewellery, perfume, combs, fans, and other items, all handmade from unique materials like tortoiseshell, silver, elder wood, porcelain, glass, and bone. Although his luck wasn't exceptional, this would no less provide an opportunity to ease Yasu's stress. Haise's eyes drifted across the arrangement as though he were trying to spot the elusive needle in the haystack.

A tap upon his shoulder had Haise turning his attention back to Yasu, who had opened his hands towards Haise to reveal a beautiful white elder wood fan with a simple crane painted on it. There was more to this piece than met the eye. Every folding section of the fan held a polished lightweight blade with a bevelled edge sharp enough to compete with any sword.

The shopkeeper spoke jovially and with a hint of surprise. "Master Emrys . . . oh my, it is a pleasure to see you. The fan you hold is the perfect gift for a young lady cultivator. Does

Master Emrys wish it to be wrapped and anonymously gifted? We deliver very quickly, and for you, absolutely free!" Haise snorted, and Yasu blushed.

"No thank you." Haise's amusement was far too obvious. "I believe the gift is for me." Yasu could no longer bear to even look in Haise's direction. Still, he held out the fan for him to take.

At the end of the handle was a delicate tassel pendant with a few pale-yellow carved beads. The piece was stunning and way beyond the price range of his own gift, but refusing it now would only hurt Yasu. He shook his head, and the massive smile spreading across his face turned quickly into joyful laughter. What a strange day it had been.

Yasu peeked up with warm eyes and relished his happiness. Snow turned to rain as Yasu smiled fondly, and raw emotion shone through his brimming tears.

Little did Haise know that this night was merely the beginning of a tragedy that would blossom into lasting misfortune and steal what little humanity remained in Dramour.

I pray my love for you transcends . . .

Now

 # Chapter 1

Haise sighed heavily. The memory forever plagued his mind. Why reminisce? He looked at the large black wolf that walked slowly beside him. Its tail waved slowly as it peered up at Haise. Wulf, his demon wolf companion, huffed as he trailed closely.

They followed a narrow path that led towards town. Streams of golden sun spilt through small openings between bamboo poles. To the side, at varying points, stood white stone spirit sculptures formed to resemble birdhouses.

Years had brought moss and cracks, so the only residents of these houses were the insects that scurried about. At least that was usually the case, but today Haise's attention caught on a movement of white. There, upon the tallest carved house, perched an elegant paper crane.

This one was far more realistic and intricate than any he'd seen before. Haise felt a strange connection to the bird and carefully reached out. The origami crane opened its delicate wings, causing the creation to take flight.

"Oh, how beautiful," Haise breathed in surprise. The ghostly bird circled him, but no sooner had it appeared than it flew out of sight. A single feather fell slowly, its white form lacked all softness as it weightlessly glided through the light.

Someone had made this and put effort into doing so, but he had no inkling as to who. The paper crane had likely been created from a person's talent, but it had shown no malice, so he dismissed it. *Anyone who could make something so graceful surely couldn't have malevolent intentions,* Haise thought, hesitantly glancing at his surroundings.

Wulf snapped it up. "Wulf! Spit that out, it's not food." The wolf gave him a look, and Haise frowned. Wulf walzed proudly out of the shade and into the sun. Haise squinted, feeling the full assault of midday. He grew increasingly tired as the walk home continued.

The street was crowded. Shouts and words extolling the virtues of various merchandise filled the air as vendors tried selling their wares to anyone brave enough to pass too close.

No matter how much interest Haise showed, glancing around at the bright and flavourful food, none would approach him for fear of the gods' retribution passing on to them. They acted as though Haise somehow cultured tribulation in his skin, transferable through touch. Even though it upset him at times, he understood why they did it, and he never blamed them for acting so cold or indifferent.

He paused a moment, his eyes seeing past the crown glass window to fixate on the hundreds of drawers holding all manner of herbs. The medicinal store was small, but the multitude of medicines it could produce was impressive. No doubt it carried exotic herbs from distant lands brought in by Vale and its black markets. He ignored the feeling of longing tinged with sadness as the smell of freshly steamed buns lured him elsewhere.

The vendor sneered. "What do you want? Come to bring ill fortune on me, eh?" The heavy, bald man wore a greasy apron a few sizes too small and looked down his nose at Haise.

"Please, just a couple of steamed buns," said Haise, trying his best to ease the tension as many eyes turned to glare at him.

The vendor tsked. "I don't serve those who live with the Forsaken One. I doubt you even have the money. Maybe if you begged on your knees, I'd give you one." Haise gently placed the few coins needed for the steamed buns on his counter. The light clinking of metal bore a foreboding air, as if it signalled a dice roll that possessed the power to determine his future.

With a scowl strong enough to curdle milk, the vendor snatched his money and promptly tossed two buns, yelling, "Scram! You're ruining business!" Haise caught one midflight but missed the other, which rolled to a stop on the cobbled road. The vendor's gratuitous actions and words were hurtful but nothing he wasn't used to.

Haise calmly bent down and carefully picked up the bun. Dirt layered the cobbled street like dust on an old book whose knowledge had long been forgotten. He held the clean bun with his teeth while brushing the dirt off the other.

He smiled and bowed his thanks, continuing towards the edge of town. He tossed the dropped steam bun to Wulf, who chomped happily at his gift.

"Being rude to me is one thing, but he didn't need to do that. Right, Wulf?" The wolf huffed between chomps as Haise took a bite of his own, relishing its warmth. The air carried off the sun-burned leaves to rest in the ever-growing sea of orange and red.

Wulf had a gargantuan appetite and stared Haise down, half whimpering, half growling in complaint at the food he still held. Haise sighed in concern for his wolf's bottomless pit of a stomach and the growing attitude that came with it.

He remembered the small pup lying injured on one of the serpentine roads connected to the market street. Haise had reached out, asking any passersby if they had recently lost a dog, but to no avail. The poor thing was starved. He gently cradled it as he returned home, praying it wasn't too late.

To his surprise, the pup turned out to be a wolf, and not only that—it was also a demon. Stubborn and unwilling to let it perish, Haise gave it a large amount of his qi. Doing so left him bedridden for many days.

Day after day, week after week, he continued to nurture the wolf. Afterwards, each time Haise tried to release it, the wolf would always return. And from the time he'd found him alone on that road to the present, Wulf had never stopped growing, nor had his stomach.

Haise gestured forwards with one hand. "Come on now, Wulf. You've had your bun. Don't be so huffy."

Wulf seemed to raise a brow at this. He sauntered ahead, annoyed that his performance brought no sympathy or extra food. Haise tailed behind as they drew ever closer to the foothills of Mount Take, where home lay nestled amongst bamboo and babbling brooks.

Soon its old wooden facade peeked through the greenery. Though small, it felt enormous compared to what they had both made do with in the past whilst travelling. It was aged by nature but strong in structure, and the refurbishing had made the house a home, bringing to it a sense of vitality and an atmosphere of warmth and comfort. After such a long time, it was nice not needing to move around so often.

Higher on the mountain and farther into the forest near a set of tiny waterfalls protruded a shaded cliff. It was Haise's favourite spot.

As they finally crested the hill, he took in the vast forest. It slept amongst the fog, as though the clouds were too lazy to join the birds, preferring to rest with the earth instead. He could think of no other place more peaceful than this as the cold air filled his lungs.

Wulf was already here, lying fast asleep under a magnificent tree, reassuring Haise that the crane had meant no harm from its visit. The sun-kissed tree seemed to defy gravity as it gripped the cliff and reached towards the heavens. *If only I dared to be as brave as you, I might've been able to . . .*

He shook his head before the thought could weigh too heavily on his mind and leapt weightlessly into a poised position near the edge, balancing effortlessly on several rocks. To increase cultivation, one must focus on one's cores.

If chosen for ascension, you were granted longevity in accordance with the three cores: your body, mind, and soul. The greater your cultivation of these aspects, the closer you came to immortality.

Training with a weapon to gain strength and stamina improved the body's ability to hold qi. Absorbing knowledge would help one learn how to focus this strength into a method that used less qi to create the same or a similar result. Practicing a talent would expand one's aptitude for molding and shaping qi. This would pave the way for qi transfer or the solidification of it.

Haise had not trained hard enough in the past, so he was determined to improve. He'd worked diligently, and after years, his mind and soul had risen to great heights. Still, no matter how hard he tried, his body remained weak, unable to gain enough qi to wield at a higher level. It didn't help that he no longer felt comfortable using a weapon. It was why he was so well versed in the lyre. He hoped fate had yet to abandon him.

Anyone who saw his lyre would say it was as pale as snow and like all other spiritual tools, qi could be channelled through it to evolve the average into the extraordinary.

Those who heard its breathtaking song and felt the warmth of its intertwining notes were gripped with awe. The name etched into it had been gouged, but although it was a simple design, its decorative carving added charm to its body.

After a moment of contemplation, a melody filled the forest, its trees shuddering from the solemn tones. The song flowed through the space effortlessly, and as notes split and joined continuously, it whispered secrets from ages long lost.

Even though his sound was impressive, Haise refused to participate in any festivals or music-related events. He no longer wished to stand amongst twinkling lights, and as for the praise of others, he only hoped to show Hiro the worth of his teachings. He wished for a simple life, one of peace that would allow him to finally hide away.

The mountain continued to shiver in response to his dancing fingers. Just as the final note took flight on the wind, his world grew silent and cold.

This particular song was one of his creations and had no power to affect others or their surroundings physically. It would attract spiritual beings only at the best of times. As far as he could recall, the summoning of malevolent entities was not his forte, especially not one of the magnitude he was sensing. Haise became uneasy: first the crane and now this.

The congregation of clouds shifted the previously red-and-golden sky to gloomy shades of mottled brown and grey. Heavy with moisture, the air condensed around Haise as if it aimed to demonstrate the inadequacies of the mortals' saying by dumping much larger creatures than merely "cats and dogs."

Warping shadows elongated into shapes that tricked the eyes, and on the rancid wind, a black feather emerged from the noxious ash cloud. Haise carefully caught it midflight, cautious not to inhale the smoke. He studied it closely within his fingertips. Smoky tendrils fell from the plume and twisted playfully around Haise's wrist. Eventually they dispersed, leaving the feather simple and without oddity.

Haise had no sooner raised a brow, wondering if it came from the new arrival, than pain surged through his arm. He had been aware of the risks in touching something oozing demonic qi, but curiosity had made him absent-minded, and the consequences of his actions now ate through his skin like a second-degree burn. A moan of agony escaped through his clenched teeth as the feather drifted to his feet.

His instrument could no longer provide the protection he now desperately wanted. Haise had never tried using one hand to play his lyre before; the spiritual tool required the steadiness of two hands and the clarity of mind to wield its full potential. He touched his finger subconsciously. A ring of paleness there made plain his loss for all to see.

He panicked, looking around nervously. Feeling cornered made him more defensive, and fear roiled his stomach. He brandished his folding fan with his nondominant hand, and it trembled terribly, his grip tight enough to make his knuckles blanch. Something cold brushed his mind, and his heart raced as a shiver ran through him.

A sweet chuckle, a fragrant aroma, and the sound of distant humming made Haise tense. All at once, he recognised the feeling of a rabbit being stalked but understood the joy of slaughter. He gingerly brought a hand to his mouth and coughed several times before he turned away from the cliff. Pain blossomed again, this time in his chest, as bright red painted his hand like a scene on canvas.

Wulf's hackles had risen, and a snarl slipped from his toothed snout as Haise called out in a hoarse voice, "What do you see, Wulf?"

Dizziness made him sway as his eyes moved towards what had caught the wolf's attention. The waterfall had stopped, its tiny droplets floating, trapped within frozen air.

It fluxed in and out of a fragmented state, as though the space itself were made by spiders who spun webs of glass, their beautiful silk refracting light at myriad angles.

A gasp escaped his lips, and he carefully approached the unearthly scene. What could allow water to act in such a manner? Was the feather somehow related?

A million thoughts crossed his mind in a matter of seconds until a distraction broke through the chaos. In a flicker of light, the white visage fluttered its delicate wings and glided weightlessly towards him as though it had never left his side, remaining completely undetected. With a bowed neck and tucked feet, the paper crane pressed its head softly against Haise's forehead between his brows.

Haise, something deep within his mind whispered. He almost keeled over as a wave of nausea hit. *Move.* It spoke earnestly as Haise clawed at his stomach. Sweat coated his body, and burning heat rushed to his head. He had considered checking his condition to find the cause of these sudden symptoms, but the need and uncontrollable urge to flee consumed his lingering thoughts.

"I . . . I need to get down . . ." Haise's lips quivered. He couldn't finish his sentence as the corners of his vision blurred and the fan almost slipped from his fingers. Wulf began to whine and tried to support Haise as he lost all sense of direction. Stumbling, he tried to find the path back down Mount Take. A white wisp appeared, blurred and fleeting. Its glowing trail enticed him to follow, so he staggered after it down the winding path as fast as his heavy legs would allow.

It vanished a couple of paces from the door of the house, and he took in a breath so he could yell out, only to find himself tipping forwards. The back steps came roaring into view, and he grimaced with squinted eyes, awaiting the inevitable, only for it never to arrive. He realised moments too late that he had passed Hiro Foxx. His teacher and now he held firmly to the back of his outer robe.

"Why are you rushing? You must be more careful and deliberate with your steps." Hiro's tone was soft but stern enough to show his seriousness. But Haise was losing consciousness in his grip and could no longer process the warning. He would have remarked that it was simply the ground's fault for being too clingy, but the void swallowed him whole. Hiro turned pale and immediately tugged him into his arms.

He pleaded to his student, "Haise. Haise, can you hear me?"

 *Chapter 2*

A murmur escaped Haise as he stirred awake with the warm lick of a tongue against his fingers. The ground beneath him was soft, and a warm glow of lantern light surrounded him. He was in Hiro's room.

His head ached from the misadventure, and pain crawled around his wrist like a swarm of ants on a march to seek food. Blood had painted his lips red, and the burn on his forearm was wrapped in a clean white cloth. *Hiro must have done this while I slept.*

Wulf's amber stare never wavered as he sat by the bed. Hiro had begun nodding off in his reading chair on the other side of the bedroom. His teacher was a worrywart and doted on him like a child. Even after he ran out of things to do for Haise, Hiro would have been too concerned to rest.

No one else saw that part of him. They see a traitor. Exiled to the outskirts of town for rejecting ascension. Some thought him modest. Most believed he'd disgraced the town and dishonoured the gods. From then on, many avoided them both.

Haise's mumbling drew Hiro straight to his feet, as though he were never truly weighed down by sleep. A few strides brought him across the room, causing the hound to vacate quickly. Wulf huffed in annoyance, but Hiro was already fretting over his student's condition and unaware or uninterested in the wolf's dismay.

"Haise, how are you feeling?" Hiro patted Haise's head, smiling fondly. Haise felt those words to the depths of his soul. He gave Hiro a smile that didn't quite make it to the corners of his eyes. "You don't seem as pale as before, but you should continue to rest. I've prepared a meal if you have the appetite."

"I'm all right now, and I appreciate the offer, but . . ." Haise trailed off when his stomach churned in complaint as the events of just hours ago came rushing back. His obvious discomfort stopped Hiro's nervous rambling before it got any worse. Yesterday had been ridiculous, but despite all that, it wasn't the worst day of his life.

Haise stroked Wulf as he told Hiro of the strange but mesmerising sight of the white crane, his trek to Mount Take, the black poisonous feather, and the bizarre scene of a waterfall refusing to fall. He thought it best not to mention the voice that crawled from the depths of his mind. He blamed the situation for his temporary insanity and felt that perhaps he had imagined it.

Hiro appeared concerned, then bafflement flashed across his face as Haise's story unfurled, but as he mentioned the feather and the crane that guided him down the mountain, something within his sensei's eyes shifted. Hiro was not often affected by what you might call bad news. He would always say, "Well, it could be worse," and then smile.

At this moment, only apprehension crossed Hiro's features, as if he saw a future where the world had lost its sun and plunged into an endless darkness that no light could ever hope to penetrate. A sense of unease encompassed Haise. Trying to ignore this feeling, he laid a hand on Hiro's shoulder, hoping to reassure his master the same way he'd done for him many times before.

Hiro removed himself to pace, only providing a small smile to Haise's gesture as he deliberated on what to do next. The exquisite flute at Hiro's waist jostled with each turn. The spiritual tool, Abore, was bestowed upon him from the Goddess of Muse even after he refused accension.

"I must leave now to speak with Delfir about this matter. Stay here. I promise not to be long." He spoke anxiously.

"No. I'm coming with you," Haise protested. If he kept acting like a child, avoiding responsibility, Hiro would keep treating him like one.

"I don't believe that's a good idea. We can discuss this more when I return," Hiro continued as he grabbed his katana. An elegant blue-and-white sword of blended metal, its razor-sharp edge lay hidden within its sheath, embellished with symbols of swirling fog. A tiny wooden carved fox hung from its wrapped handle, a tribute to the Clan of Lakin.

"No. Once you return, you won't divulge anything in order to 'keep me safe,' as you often say."

"I could make you a promise."

"Promises can be broken, Hiro." Haise held his ground, narrowing his eyes in an unwavering stare. He might not be as strong as Hiro, who was currently his master, but they shared a past that placed them on equal footing.

Hiro sighed deeply. It was obvious where Wulf got his stubbornness from. Hiro couldn't prevent Haise from coming, and time was of the essence. "That is true. All right then, meet me outside once you're ready."

Haise got out of bed gingerly, testing his footing before grabbing his satchel and fixing his clothing as best he could to appear at least somewhat presentable.

He felt bad about not eating Hiro's meal, but the food would not be wasted. He grabbed the pot and placed it on the floor.

"Wulf!" he whispered urgently. "Don't let Hiro know I gave this to you." The wolf was quite content, lapping away, as Haise left the room. He would make it up to his master somehow, but that would have to wait.

Hiro had already started on his way, but since he hadn't travelled far, Haise was easily able to make up the distance. The sun still had not fully risen, so the moon's tiny rays and residual glow lit up the moisture created by an overnight drizzle.

Thankfully, the wind wasn't too strong, but what it lacked in speed, it made up for in temperature. Haise and his companion's breath was visible as they spoke in hushed tones to one another, the town growing more prominent as they approached. Since they lived close by, it wasn't long before they hit the outer markets. The glow from store lanterns breached the fogged windows, creeping onto the cobblestone road.

There were more people than expected out and about at this hour, preparing for the day, though no customers roamed the streets like they did during the bustling evenings.

Past the markets on the main street stood the stalwart gates of Delfir's residence, the House of Serpents. Surrounded by a decorative stone wall, the land he occupied wasn't much to some, but to Haise, it was a touch excessive.

Having grown up with less than most, he understood the love of luxury but also found it unseemly to flaunt it. For this reason and another, more annoying one, Haise wasn't particularly fond of his lordship.

Hiro and Delfir had known each other long before Hiro arrived here in Helmbi with Haise in tow. The two almost seemed like family, as though they had been kin in a past life and were now enjoying each other's company again.

His master could solve most issues but always went to Delfir when troubled by something he couldn't cope with alone. The fact that they were standing at the gate of serpents confirmed the seriousness of the situation.

More people were milling about the gates than expected, as if they wished for an audience with the patriarch too but were somewhat apprehensive to come forwards. One guard stood stiff-backed, wearing clothes that hung too loosely. Regardless, he tried his best to give the impression of being reliable and capable of his duties. The other straightened from a relaxed posture to one of annoyance and stepped closer to cross his spear with that of the stiff guard. Hiro and Haise's approach had been effectively blocked.

"Halt. State your business, sirs, or be on your way." The relaxed guard spoke with as much enthusiasm as a tired ass, and the other seemed as though he were trying to be impassive, but the more he tried, the more uncomfortable he looked.

The black attire both guards proudly wore boasted the embroidered orange insignia of the House of Serpents on the chest and sleeves.

Hiro said earnestly, "I seek an audience with your patriarch. It is of great importance and quite urgent."

The stiff guard made Hiro aware of his prospects of being seen, saying that many civilians had the same request and the patriarch grew weary. The other stared Haise down and grinned with malintent, as if realising an opportunity that could not be wasted.

"Well, well, if it isn't our little bad omen. Have you come to smite us? Too weak to wield a weapon like a real man?" His words dripped with arrogance and amusement as he swung his spear towards Haise. "No matter of yours is important to the likes of our patriarch," he scoffed, apparently unaware that his words were having little effect, for behind him now stood a stern and elegant woman. She lifted a brow, suggesting much doubt in the man's aptitude for reading the room.

The stiff guard noticed her and somehow became stiffer when withdrawing back into position. His spear upright at his side and his eyes downcast, he stood motionless, as though afraid of the attention of this mysterious woman.

She lightly cleared her throat, and with this single action, the once-relaxed man's face drained of all colour. As he went to step aside to take up the post, she spoke firmly. "No need. Grab your possessions and leave. You have been dismissed on my patriarch's orders." His face, previously lacking all life, turned bright red, followed by a myriad of other colours as he hastily removed himself, as though both furious and deeply humiliated.

"Master Foxx, it is a pleasure to see you again. I have been expecting you," she said, then paused. Turning to Haise, she bowed. With a pleasant smile, she spoke with an air of kindness quite different from her previous demeanour of cold indifference. "You may call me Kina, Master Alsta. It is also a pleasure to meet you."

Haise quickly acknowledged her greeting. "Just Haise is fine."

Straightening, she glanced back at Hiro. "I'll seat you in the main quarters and have the patriarch meet you there. I apologise for how our guards have treated you both," she said, also promising to reiterate to the guards her and the patriarch's position in regard to chosen family. She then politely addressed the crowd that had gathered to watch the confrontation. "All your issues will be heard by the patriarch later this afternoon. Please take comfort in this and continue your day as usual." Gradually, they dispersed, and she requested that Haise and Hiro follow her.

She led them along one of the patterned stone pathways that stretched in various directions, most undoubtedly arriving at entrances to the interconnected buildings. The largest led straight ahead to a great hall filled with furniture of the finest craftsmanship, drapery bearing the same serpent emblem as the guards' uniforms, and carved pillars that bore the weight of slanted roofs. Upon them perched serpentine dragon sculptures that flowed and curved as though frozen in the midst of a dance.

Above the doorway to the hall, etched into the wood, was its name: *Hall of Subdual.* The structure was flawless, from its outer design to its grand interior. For that reason, it demanded centre stage. If any high-ranking officials or royalty visited, an impressive banquet would be held there.

Dotted throughout the space were pots of flowers and well-maintained garden beds. They all came together to create a dazzling atmosphere of colour in the rising light. The tapping of carved bamboo and running water were the only sounds that could be heard. *I may dislike Delfir, but I have to admit, his gardens are quite peaceful,* Haise thought.

Kina promptly guided them into some smaller, luxurious quarters. Before departing, she assured them the patriarch would arrive in a few moments.

Now that it was just the two of them again, Haise took the chance to look around. The room was pristine, with minimal decoration. A low table with four zabutons on a rush tatami stood within its centre. The place smelt fresh and pleasantly sweetened by a vase of flowers, which rested on a long, tall table against the wall. They held firm to their beauty, eagerly competing with the magnificent painting on the wall above their lofty display. Haise could have sworn the figures within the painted scene moved and the fire that raged through its hills licked the canvas, its edges smouldering as the land was consumed.

He was about to ask Hiro what event was captured here when he heard a voice behind him say, "A painting of the Great Heavenly War, so cataclysmic that it created new valleys and destroyed mountains when fire ravaged the land, holy weapons were lost, and mythical creatures were near extinction." Haise flinched in surprise and spun around towards the owner of this voice, who moved as silent as a snake on the hunt for mice.

Before him stood Lord Dameon Delfir. About Hiro's height, he had straight, dark, partially woven hair that rested on his black robe. The cuffs bore tiny delicate patterns in gold that swirled with purpose, as if they were a divination written in an ancient, lost tongue.

His face seemed tired, as though he'd been awake most of the night, but his eyes shone with life. His pellucid irises reflected colourful light upon various fractured surfaces, like flawless crystals shaped for fine jewellery. This man was the only person Haise had ever met who was never pinned by Hiro's words, never swayed nor cornered.

There was a flicker of delight in his smile as he continued. "The Heavenly Emperor came down to the mortal realm to banish all evil back to the ghost realm and killed the Ghost King in the process. The humans prospered once more, but the war had destroyed all borders. Food, art, attire, and many other unique traditions were melded together."

Delfir exhaled smoke from an ornate pipe so old it wouldn't have been out of place in a time before the war. Tendrils snaked through the air as if responding to unspoken commands, even slithering around Haise's neck. Slowly, Delfir retreated to the table and took a seat on one of the zabutons. Glancing back, he gestured for a stunned Haise to do the same before continuing.

"Every town built new temples to worship one or more of the gods in gratitude for having protected them, but the heavens had lost so many. To bring back strength to the heavenly realm, the deities held a test. Those who could prove themselves worthy joined their ranks. You know this as the Festival of Celestial Arts. A bygone tradition thanks to *that man*." He sneered at the last part, as though just the thought of this person infuriated him.

Haise had known all this even before Hiro thought to teach him. The deities' test was something his mother would mention quite often. She would tell him every night that if he ever got strong enough, he too would join the gods. Unfortunately, like most stories, it was a fairy tale with an ending far too perfect for reality.

"Delfir, please. Enough of the history lesson," Hiro interrupted before Delfir thought it amusing to continue.

"Hmm, so impatient. We haven't spoken in so long. Why not savour the moment?" Delfir softly complained.

Just then, a maid entered the room from a corridor behind them and placed a tea set and a plate of petits four on the table, after which she bowed deeply and left.

"Don't you think it's too early for this kind of indulgence?" Hiro raised a brow to Delfir, who promptly took a sweet and bit into it with sheer pleasure.

"Absolutely not, my Little Fox. Life is much too short to be unhappy." His smile was filled with something more than satisfaction. Hiro sighed and shook his head slightly, as if displeased, but he said nothing more. Haise, on the other hand, considered whether such an indulgence was truly a bad thing. In all honesty, it looked quite delicious.

"I have come to seek your vast library and knowledge on ghosts. I must know why such an enormous malicious aura suddenly took root on Mount Take, and why it targeted Haise." Hiro's demeanour wavered. His jaw clenched as his brows furrowed with worry.

"And why it vanished just as quickly?" Delfir spoke as though stating a fact rather than a question, as if he were finishing a thought that Hiro had yet to voice. Negative emotions didn't often sway Hiro. His teachings consisted of calming and gentle techniques, so there was no room for anger or annoyance.

"Mm. You know you have yet to greet me properly." Delfir pouted.

Hiro became placid once more and responded solemnly, "Please excuse my ill etiquette. It's a pleasure to see you again, Delfir. How have you been faring?"

Delfir smirked and let out a chuckle under his breath at Hiro's immediate and obedient response.

"Well enough."

This back-and-forth banter was one of those previously mentioned reasons for Haise's lack of fondness. He considered that perhaps it would have been better for him to stay at home, but it was a fleeting thought, since he was determined not to be removed again from a situation involving himself.

"I thought we talked about this already, my Little Fox. You should be calling me Dameon." Delfir winked at Hiro.

Haise was very determined.

Chapter 3

Seated leisurely on the zabuton closest to the open shoji, Delfir obscured the view into the gardens beyond. Hiro finished explaining the events that Haise had previously recounted, and Delfir examined the burn.

"Hmm, this injury is strange. Make sure you keep an eye on it and ensure it stays clean. Though I'm sure you're perfectly aware of that." He directed the last part to Haise, then turned to Hiro. "And yes, such a disturbance was felt even this far from the mountain, and those anxious about the effects have been expressing their worries at all hours of the night. Alas, I can only console them and grant them peace of mind by insisting that all will be well."

He glanced at Haise thoughtfully, then continued speaking to Hiro. "However, I don't believe the aura was from Soul Seeker. The new Ghost King was present to a degree, based on the appearance of your little white crane, but if he decided to attack your student, he would already be dead. The Ghost King is not above making grand displays of power but never targets people without good reason. He mainly attacks temples or worshipped statues of dubiously ascended gods."

Good reason? So the King of Death has a conscience?

Haise had been unaware that the Ghost King held two titles and had never thought to ask. Curious now, he repeated the name. "Soul Seeker?"

Delfir turned back to him, his crystal eyes twinkling again as he exclaimed, "Yes! A name given by the people, and oh how well it suits him." He leaned towards Haise, his excitement infectious, as though he'd been waiting eons for someone to ask him anything so that the vastness of his knowledge could stretch its tired legs.

"It is said that when the Soul Seeker strikes, mountains bend to his mercy and red washes the land, forcing the heavens to cry. After each incident, a white paper crane can be found amongst the flames and ash, the crane somehow untouched by its heat and not affected by the tortures of time. Forever he searches for a single soul. Some say it's his other half. Others say he looks for his lost essence, but I believe it's a past lover."

At this, Haise felt a sense of absolute bewilderment. The story brought to mind the preposterous notion of a cat nurturing a mouse. Catching on quickly to the change in Haise's expression, Delfir continued, "That's right. A lover lost to the passage of time, perhaps even before he became the demonic king, but of course, it's only a theory."

Hiro looked at Haise thoughtfully and said, "Some towns also refer to him as the King with a Thousand Faces. Others simply call him Akuma, a malevolent fire spirit."

Delfir looked pleased that Hiro had joined in, but such intriguing talk wouldn't get them closer to solving their problem.

"Your reasoning as to why it isn't the Ghost King leaves me doubtful. Do you have any other ideas about who or what that entity was?" Hiro questioned.

"No, unfortunately. Given the presence, however, you're dealing with at least a sublime-class being, one level under the calamity class seen during the war. But at least we can be sure it was targeting your student." He smiled as if he weren't giving them the worst news possible.

Haise had met only one calamity-class being before, and it was no surprise they called him the god of gods. With training, one could surpass one's limits and increase one's class, but as it stood, Haise had only recently passed mediocre, which was considered the lowest level, where you would expect most children to be.

Following that was the intermediate level, which was where Haise now sat. The next level was split in two for the demonic and the heavenly—the sublime and the transcendent, respectively. Nine times out of ten, people were born with a higher aptitude for either demonic qi or heavenly qi. Concentrating on whichever qi it was made it easier to excel but generally led to a weakness in the other, and that was why the classes had split. Haise knew Hiro was transcendent but was unsure about Lord Delfir.

By the time a being became a member of the calamity class, this distinction was pointless, since their power could create rifts that would destroy the fabric of the world or be used to craft something from nothing.

"Since the king of all ghosts was likely present, he would know what's after you," Delfir suggested after a pause. Haise's heart sank at the idea of being hunted, though he thought that perhaps this was what he deserved. His dream of a peaceful life drifted away on the wind like sand off a crumbling castle.

"You are suggesting we walk into the depths of the ghost realm and question the most dangerous being in there, then wait expectantly for an answer." Hiro spoke doubtfully.

"Believe it or not, my Little Fox, he is not as unreasonable as you think. For a price, he would divulge or undertake various things." Delfir smirked and, with mischief in his voice, finished by purring, "Within reason."

Haise had heard of this before, even though he had been unaware of the king's other names. He did, however, know a couple of other well-known facts. Out of all the previous kings, it was he who had brought wicked laughter to the halls of his throne, turning pain into pleasure and all disdain into esteem.

If you were brave enough to travel to the ghost realm by seeking out the pathways, you could ask him for anything and everything. Nothing was off-limits, but there was a catch. The price was ambiguous, and most were deterred by that alone.

You could ask for a cure to your child's illness at the cost of your village burning down, or you might wish to become a nobleman only to have years of your life stripped away. The more you asked for, the higher the cost.

Haise was sure there were still some things even the Ghost King could not accomplish, and to reveal this truth could place his position of power at risk of being usurped.

Most humans, most ghosts, and the occasional god would request small feats, but there had been recorded incidences in which core essences had been given as payment. Considered a last resort, this was an extremely dangerous act for any who participated. In most cases, death was chosen instead.

Haise had wanted to go before, but he was one of the discouraged. He had nothing the king would find interesting and couldn't pay with his core essence. But the possibility of such an opportunity was one he couldn't dismiss: a chance to ask what had happened to his dear friend. *Yasu, are you still alive . . . or am I just a fool for hoping?*

Hiro cleared his throat, breaking Haise's thoughts. "If you believe he will help, then I trust your word, but if the price is unreasonable . . ." He trailed off in concern, his brows furrowed.

"Let me tell you a secret." Delfir paused as if for dramatic effect, at which Haise unintentionally leaned in slightly, awaiting some form of heavenly knowledge to spill from his lips. What he said next surprised him. "He hasn't left the ghost realm in several years."

It was absurd to think that a man of his stature and presence would prefer to stay homebound, and Haise's doubt showed.

"Hmm, there is no way to convince you, I know. Still, I doubt you will find trouble with his trade. Bring something along that is unique. He enjoys simple pleasures, so I'm sure you'll find a way." Delfir spoke as though a little hurt, but his attitude shifted when he reached for the tea.

The hot amber liquid poured from the spout into a little yunomi patterned with soft browns and creams that mimicked the strata of mountains. A small splash of milk made the liquid creamy, and sugar helped to sweeten the brew. He took a sip as it steamed, which further spread its strong spicy aroma. The scent was exotic. Most likely the tea had been imported from Vale.

Delfir returned the cup and seemed to consider his thoughts until finally turning away to face the gardens.

"There is something you should be aware of before you set out." His voice deepened, becoming amiable and sincere, although his posture contradicted his tone. "Ghosts are humans after death, but they don't usually resemble their original forms in life. Demons are different. They are neither alive nor dead and possess the body of a beast. Even though they are dissimilar, both can be tricked by using one method. So I have a parting gift for each of you."

With ethereal grace, two women emerged from the corridor. Approaching the wooden table from behind, they were beyond silent, as though they didn't even exist. Their strange presence caused Haise to shiver, hairs rising on his skin. Leaning down, the women each placed a unique decorative kitsune mask on the low-lying table.

The one resting beside Haise was white with red markings encircling each feature, including the insides of its ears. Below the left ear hung two bells from a red string tied into a bow.

Hiro's mask was similar to his, give or take a few markings, with pointier ears and angular eyes. It also had bells and a tied woven string with a couple of beads at its ends.

Delfir's voice filled the space once more with an ominous presence. "Please take these. They will hide your aura and qi. Your existence will become insignificant, and most will pass you by without even realising you were there. They won't protect you from Akuma, but they should at least hide you well enough amongst the lesser ghosts and demons."

Hiro bowed his head in thanks, but Delfir remained unmoving. With such stillness, it was as though he'd been paralysed by one of the many venomous snakes throughout the ever-encroaching wilderness. Haise went to thank the women for delivering the gifts, but to his surprise, both had vanished.

"You must never remove your mask; remember, do not trust your senses. Everything within the ghost realm will try to deceive you, so question your actions, for they may not be your own."

"You worry too much, Delfir. We will be fine," Hiro assured him. Delfir shifted sideways and glanced back at Hiro. A hint of pain crossed his face.

"And you worry too little. By the way, you should be careful taking the forest path. Something has been amiss there for the last few days. Unfortunately, I haven't had the time to investigate nor send anyone to do so on my behalf." Concern pressed wrinkles into his otherwise flawless skin.

"I promise you, we'll be safe," Hiro insisted, but the words, like before, didn't seem to reach Delfir's ears, as though the weight of his assurance was as light as air. Haise was almost amused as he watched Delfir treat Hiro the same way Hiro treated him.

"Kina, please escort them to the stables."

Kina appeared suddenly, as though she had been there the whole time, hidden within the shadows. Although this warning made Haise apprehensive, he was happy to leave, as the silent appearances and disappearances were starting to freak him out. *Perhaps this is why they're called the Serpent Clan.*

Hiro and Haise politely excused themselves, taking the kitsune masks with them. Delfir raised the pipe to his lips once more, and from within the smoke, he whispered, "Oh, old friend, where did I go wrong?" Haise glanced back before leaving as a woeful sigh escaped Delfir's lips. "Be careful . . ." A wisp of smoke snaked its way down the corridor, as though trying to deliver his message to Hiro, but dissolved into nothing before it could reach its destination.

The morning light bathed the room in a warm glow as Haise left to the soft sound of Delfir murmuring, "Please."

Chapter 4

The stable was towards the front of the estate and nestled against the corner walls, almost opposite where they had been just moments ago. Kina stopped to address what appeared to be someone hunched over inside one of the stalls.

"Vallas, these are the gentlemen our patriarch mentioned. Treat them well and make sure they get there in one piece."

"Yes, my lady, O great and noble one." A deep laugh resounded from the stall, but instead of rude mockery, it carried the tone of familiar banter.

"Delfir requested that I inform you should the entity reappear. Word will be sent to you via messenger bird. Safe travels, Master Foxx, Master Alsta." Kina spoke succinctly while maintaining her polite demeanour before she swiftly left the two behind.

Haise and Hiro turned their attention to Vallas, who approached them slowly while running a hand down one of the beasts. She stood taller than Haise, with a toned muscular body, a sword at her side, two crossing short swords on her back, and a dagger sheathed on her chest. These weren't the only weapons in her possession, and Haise believed there would be more hidden from view. Her smile shone as four black wings flared from behind, the top pair larger than the bottom two. Pieces of black-and-silver armour adorned various areas of her body, like the bracers on her lower arms and the greaves encasing her legs to the middle of her boots.

She appeared more than capable of defeating any enemy, even without a weapon. Haise knew the spirit-kissed disease had become an inherited trait. To this day, plenty still hated the appearance of those who bore it and discriminated against them because of it. Fortunately, the genes that gave humans a more beastly form were slowly becoming a more natural phenomenon and thus more openly accepted. Each case Haise saw still saddened him, even though such a long time had passed since the outbreak.

Based on Vallas's demeanour, Haise knew his pity would not be welcomed, so he smiled meekly as she assessed the two with the confidence of a soldier born and bred for the harshest conditions.

Hiro greeted her smile with one in return. "It's a pleasure to see you again, Vallas."

"Aaargh! Hiro, it is good to see you too. How's solitude treating you? I thought you'd have tried to make at least one friend here, but you've forgotten your promise already, huh?" She laughed boisterously as she walked over, patting Hiro's arm several times. "At least you have the pip-squeak." She raised a brow at Haise. There was a glint of hope and sadness in those eyes of hers, but they quickly sharpened when she reached for the dagger on her chest.

Within seconds, she had struck a pose and sent the blade flipping through the air, slicing at the currents. The blade ripped its way towards Haise with incredible speed. Hiro could easily have stopped it, but his master didn't move an inch, so Haise twisted.

The sound of singing metal rang in his ear. Reaching up, he breathed out gently, grabbing the handle of the careening blade with his good hand, and as the world slowed, he spun, throwing it cleanly back.

His long battle with hesitation had ended many years ago—or at least he'd hoped it had. The fear crawling around his chest about hitting his mark told a different story. The dagger flew directly at Vallas, but with a happy huff, she tilted her head, hair whipping up as it missed. *That was too close.*

Haise breathed a sigh of relief at his failure as the dagger buried itself in the ground behind her. Vallas laughed deeply.

"You taught him well, Hiro," she stated sincerely, only to add, "Shame his dance is no match for mine." Her amusement was not that of mockery but rather enjoyment and gratitude that he had responded so well. Vallas continued to chuckle as she rejoined the beasts in the stable to prepare for the journey ahead. Haise was confused. Nevertheless, he was grateful no one had gotten hurt.

"She has her reasons," Hiro said, trying to excuse her actions. "You did well to counter that."

In response, Haise squeezed out a strange noise that could have been related to a thank-you.

It wasn't too long before the wagon was ready and pulled out onto the main street, awaiting the boarding of its guests. The animal pulling the cart was similar to a lizard and called a nimako. They were common in this area and easy to tame with food. If treated with respect and proper care, they were relatively loyal. The creature's front legs rose higher than its back legs, allowing it to stand as tall as the average man, but it weighed significantly more. Its colouring was a mottled black and grey with touches of green.

Its thick tail lazily moved about the dirt, rubbing a few scales loose. A nimako's bite could crush limbs, but it would have been much worse if it had any teeth. As it closely watched Haise's movements, a tongue slipped out to lick its eye free of dust and other irritants.

Vallas's shout cut through Haise's focus on the nimako. "Hey, come on, or I'll leave you behind!"

The wagon's four beams held up a sloped gabled roof covering its potential cargo, and with a white cloth rolled and tied beneath each edge, it could keep passengers shielded from most of the elements. The dark wooden edge had been carved with special attention to its natural grains. The etchings illustrated a phoenix's cycle on repeat. Hiro extended his hand for Haise to grab hold of, and with a tug, he boarded the wagon.

"Beautiful," Haise breathed. The exquisite artistry would keep this well-known tale of rebirth ensnared within the grain for years to come.

"Some of my best work." Vallas fondly patted the wood, as though memories of her past were stored within and simply touching the wagon sent a wealth of joy rushing through her. "I also made those masks of yours, so don't go breaking or losing them. I won't be making you another."

"Thank you. I promise I'll take good care of it," Haise blurted, turning pink soon after his loud proclamation. Hiro chuckled as Vallas yelled and threw the reins down on the wood, causing the nimako to rise from its rested position. At a quick walking pace, it raced down the street out onto the road Hiro and Haise had traversed just this morning.

As they passed Mount Take, Hiro turned to Haise. "Are you sure you wish to make this journey? To venture to Norval is to pass through Falk. Will this not burden your thoughts?"

His fingers twitched with something between nervousness and anger. "Yes, I'll be fine." He wasn't about to dredge up the past right now and let it haunt his days more than it already did. He reached down to his lyre and gently plucked a string.

The noise vibrated through the air with a ghostly hum, and the qi sent out with the note added a layer of complexity to the single sound. In the next second, Wulf was bounding down the road, his fur whipping around as he tore through the breeze, kicking up dust clouds in his wake. He hunched down just as his features gained more detail, and with a flick of his ears, he leapt onto the wagon straight through the open rear. The wagon buckled under his weight as the wood creaked in complaint. The wolf settled fast, taking up more than half the space underneath the sheltered section.

The road grew more and more unstable the farther they travelled from town. The cobblestones slowly broke away into compact dirt, and long grass erupted between the cracks as though nature had no more patience to wait to receive back what had been stolen. Amongst the fight for ground lay something astonishing, and its unusuality caught Haise's eye as the wagon slowed, approaching the forest path.

Chasing the road towards the forest were small, scattered patches of flourishing greenery. Each was speckled with flowers and clouded by fine dust, which shimmered and emanated a flow of energy.

"Heavenly qi . . . ?" Haise mumbled softly with furrowed brows. *Whoever this came from must not be able to contain their qi properly.* He and his companions were after an entity that exuded an enormous demonic aura, so although the scene was interesting, there didn't seem to be a reason to bother the others about it.

He quietly watched the qi swirl like the undercurrents of rolling waves, crashing into flower stems and spreading through the grass as if it were beach sands. The wisps of qi veered off the trail into gatherings of tiny unique sculptures that dotted sections of the ground.

It was then that darkness engulfed the wagon, and his mind shifted from distraction to attention. The cool, damp forest closed around them, its canopy becoming a wash of dark orange and yellow. It should have allowed scattered light to illuminate the fallen debris, but all remained unlit.

The path drew on as they passed logs, rocks, the odd birch tree, and a stone plaque, but it never seemed to end. Haise yawned as he slid off his seat and leaned back into Wulf on the floor, a huff of hello the only sign he was awake.

His unease worsened with every passing moment. It had been too long, the path too great a length. Haise could tell that everyone felt wary, and the silence they had been riding in began to itch at him.

"I don't remember the trail within this forest being quite this long," Haise ventured.

"You're right. It has taken longer than expected. Something is off." Hiro scanned the trees as he spoke. Amidst their hushed tones, Vallas perked up.

"There! A stone plaque!" She pointed to the structure that gave the city beyond the forest its name. The rock should have raised his hopes, but Haise had an inkling he'd seen it before. He shook his head to discourage thoughts of misfortune. It was too soon to assume the worst. He could be mistaken.

Hiro's suspicions seem to linger, and he scrutinised the stone as if he expected the rock to awaken and morph into a golem. They pressed on, passing the time with idle conversation and the odd nap or two. Haise began to wonder if they would make the next village before nightfall. That is, if night hadn't fallen already.

He noticed a large stone standing to the side of the road, cracked and worn with age. He had definitely seen it before, its face marked with the old heavenly symbols for *north* and *valley*. They were no closer to Norval. They had somehow looped around. Twice.

Chapter 5

For several moments, they held still enough to feel their hearts beating, as though something were waiting a mere hairbreadth beyond the veil of sight.

Vallas narrowed her eyes and, taking initiative, jumped from the wagon to take a closer look. Haise shouldn't have relaxed so quickly before, and a simple glance at Hiro confirmed his thoughts. The disturbance Delfir had mentioned was a domain barrier. This was a trap, but was it meant for them, or were they in the wrong place at the wrong time?

"We have been caught within a domain," Hiro announced. Vallas kicked a stone in frustration. It shot through the air and struck a tree with enough force to embed itself deep within the trunk and cause fractures to radiate from the impact.

"If we are to get free, we will have to locate the crux of this domain before it gets any stronger," Hiro continued after he pulled his attention away from the new tiny hollow in the tree. This was going to take a while. There was no hard-and-fast rule for escaping a domain.

"I know Delfir warned us about this, but to think it would be something so troublesome . . ." Haise said quietly. "I don't have a good feeling about this."

"Arrgh, no need to worry so much." Vallas spoke as she regained control of the reins and her temper, but there was a stillness to her that gave her uplifting tone a subtle dark side. With a flick of the wrist, the wagon pulled off again towards their unreachable destination.

Domains were areas owned or held hostage by individuals or a group. There were only four known ways to escape a domain. The first was to kill its caster. The second involved the death of all those trapped. The third entailed destruction of the crux, and the fourth, most unlikely situation was that the holder let you go straight through.

It was more possible for Haise to grow wings and fly than for the latter to be on the holder's mind. He wasn't going to try his luck, because he didn't feel like dying today. It would be far too painful, and wearing the dead as a ghost didn't tickle his fancy.

Their only hope of getting out of here lay with either the crux's destruction or the domain holder's death. The crux and the domain holder were often found together, since the holder poured qi into the crux, and that item then held the domain in place. It would benefit the trio if they were separate, since finding the holder would be impossible unless it chose to show itself.

Haise hoped desperately that it was not a veil walker. The veil was an unused space imperceivable to anyone apart from some demons, any calamity-class being, or those who trained extensively to use it. A demon that could hunt from the veil was more challenging to perceive and even more difficult to track. He'd have Wulf to help with this type of attack, but he still hoped it was simply an aggressive ghost who lacked the mental capacity to understand its actions and had only rage fuelling its motives.

"Hmm." Hiro broke the silence. "Turn here." Haise surveyed the area, scrutinising any and every object that could offer details as to why the path piqued Hiro's interest. *What exactly has he seen?*

They said seeing was believing; Haise would say feeling was also believing. The sudden ominous pressure in the air was foreboding, and although nothing was visible, he knew it would be unwise to disregard its existence.

The demonic energy was abnormally strong. Though it wasn't powerful enough to disorient them, it still warranted an investigation. It could indicate the position of the crux.

The path became barely wide enough to accommodate the wagon, its wheels enduring the hardships of uneven soil. A bright, glowing light slipped past the trees, escaping its creator to illuminate the shadows, which hid in every nook and cranny amongst the debris of nature.

A magnificent small building came into view, its windows overflowing with odds and ends, the types of items that randomly disappeared around one's house and were never found again. Clothing of all sorts, necklaces and rings, strings and strings of beads, and half-used candles were only a few of these objects.

The place boasted a multitude of smaller sections on its sides and top, creating variously shaped roofing. The front protruded into a glass-enclosed sitting area with at least a dozen fluffy pillows. It gave off vibes more similar to those of a secret restaurant than a cheap gift store.

To the left, a banner reading *Wotknots* clung to the building, and to the right, a wooden door with a lightbox announced its open status. Haise held his breath as it swayed in the slight breeze that had snaked through the dense forest. The stability of the structure was unlike that of a typical building. The whole thing resembled a perilously balanced tower strung together with a thin cord.

The closer they drew, the more ethereal the structure appeared. Haise thought the sight was magical. Wulf snarled at a flicker of movement behind the glass. The nimako stopped in its tracks, head pulled back, unwilling to move any closer.

Vallas jumped off to soothe the creature with mumbled words and gentle strokes. By the time Haise and Hiro stepped down from the cart, its wild eyes had grown calm, and it stood at attention. Haise told Wulf to wait as they approached the door, and it creaked open of its own volition.

It was like walking into another world. The space inside was much larger than it should have been, but it was more the atmosphere that gave this place its otherworldly feel.

There were shelves upon shelves of rare artefacts, pottery, jewellery, forged items, scrolls of old knowledge, accessories, and more. The back wall was covered in tiny drawers, some labelled, some hanging open, but most displayed decorative keyholes, which suggested that higher-value items were held within. Precarious book piles dotted the area, and at the centre of it all, towards the back of the room, stood a large desk, and behind it was the owner of this strange store.

"Grrrreetings." It spoke with a toothy grin. "Pray tell, what brings you here? Lost?" It cackled in amusement. The creature reminded Haise of a weasel with the colours and fluffy tail of a fox, but it walked and talked like a human. As it came out from behind the desk, Haise could see it was wearing a vest with a white shirt and a pair of pants with no shoes. Haise was so completely confused. He had never seen such an unusual being in his life.

"We are not lost, demon," Hiro bluntly stated, which surprised Haise even further. He had assumed demons could possess only a single animal and were unable to manipulate their form. He had thought Wulf was incredibly unique when it came to the demon race.

What stood before him now was something else, something twisted. Admittedly, its grin was unsettling, yet it didn't frighten him. He mentally grappled with the urge to see if its tail was as soft as it looked.

Its smile grew more prominent as it giggled again. "Are you sure? How should I help you? Looking for anything in particular?"

Haise narrowed his eyes at the demon's persistence. No doubt the comment was a simple ploy to mess with their heads, so he should avoid fixating on its randomness.

He had no idea what the crux looked like, but that was the same for his companions as well. No one could answer that question successfully.

Haise racked his brain for an excuse; any would do. If he asked directly about the crux and the weasel was somehow involved, it would be the end of their trip and possibly their lives.

Instead of answering truthfully, Haise said, "I'm looking for a gift, Mr Weasel." The other two glanced at him, but he held fast, hoping to fool the demon. It narrowed its eyes, as though discerning something from Haise's body language, but only rebutted with, "It's Mr Binkle." He paused to ponder, then continued, "Who's it for?"

Haise hadn't thought this far ahead. He'd never considered that Mr Binkle would ask such a question, and the fact that he hadn't made him feel stupid. His mind raced for an answer.

He could say Hiro or even Vallas, but that would be too awkward, so he said, "An old friend I haven't seen in many years." His thoughts had settled on the image of the boy he remembered back in Dramour as a child. He tried not to focus on what had happened to him but rather on the smile he wore when they were together.

This memory made him sad, but not the kind that could cause tears to fall. Instead, it was deep-seated, leaving behind an empty space filled with bittersweet moments.

"I see." Mr Binkle's face shone with more curiosity than before, something unspoken seeming to shift behind his animalistic eyes. Haise recalled what Delfir had said earlier today, and it spilt quietly from his lips.

"Something unique, a strange and interesting object rarely seen."

Those pools of darkness captured his stare. Within their abyss, ghostly hands reached out to grasp his mind and steal precious thoughts, violating his hidden world.

"The crux I have not, though you've come to the right place . . . perhaps this is fate's doing." Mr Binkle snickered at the revelation, at which Haise blanched. He had hoped the feeling of being invaded was merely that, but the demon had a privilege no being should. Haise flicked his gaze down, away from the talking weasel. The break in contact helped him clear his mind, but it was short-lived.

Vallas drew two daggers, and Hiro stepped back, one hand at the ready and the other resting on Abore. Mr Binkle randomly vanished and reappeared in multiple locations. The sight was frightening, but Haise watched in awe as the weasel slipped in and out of the veil with ease. It allowed him to walk from one spot to another, avoiding all objects between.

"Hmm . . . where is it? Where did I put it?" Mr Binkle mumbled to himself, either unaware of his guests' unease or feeling absolutely no threat from their display of such meagre strength. The weasel made a sound similar to an *ah* as it clung to the back wall, its claws hooked on open drawers. He held a key he had no doubt collected during the search.

Haise hadn't noticed how quiet it was until the click of a lock and the scraping of wood filled the space. The weasel withdrew a slender silver chain from the box and leapt towards him, causing everyone but Haise to tense. Mr Binkle's smile had yet to fade as his fingers unfurled to reveal a stunning necklace.

Silver links delicately joined together, creating a polished chain that led to a black stone held in place by an intricate wire wrap. The gem seemed to hum with life, and within was a faint glow, as though its core was so incredibly hot it remained a burning liquid, trying and failing to eat its way out.

"This looks far too expensive. Maybe something a little more mediocre?" Haise smiled sheepishly. He hadn't felt any demonic energy pouring out of this object or any others, nor had he felt anything unusual coming from Mr Binkle since stepping inside. Though it was unfortunate, the weasel wasn't deceiving them; this place did not contain the crux after all, and Hiro would have also sensed this by now.

"A trade is fine with me," Mr Binkle stated. Haise, however, was still in need of an interesting item to exchange for information. *Surely Akuma would find this unique.*

"I doubt we have anything you would like," Hiro said, more relaxed than before, but his hand remained atop his flute. The weasel considered this and then stepped closer to Haise.

"Your hairpin."

"My hairpin . . ." Haise wavered. He knew it was important to acquire the necklace, but the hairpin was a gift from his mother, and he couldn't easily part with it. Sensing this shift, the weasel cocked his head. He now knew the hairpin's worth, and as if he relished taking candy from a child, he would enjoy taking something so precious. But as the weasel reached out, Vallas broke his fixation on Haise by unsheathing the knife on her chest and offering it up instead.

The blade reflected the candlelight in the room, showing off its dark steel. The clip-point blade's spine tapered in thickness to a recurve in line with its central axis, and the false edge had been sharpened to increase its piercing effectiveness. The knife was made to kill, and the idea of obtaining it enthralled the weasel.

No longer interested in the hairpin, the weasel agreed eagerly to the trade, overjoyed with his new knife. Mr Binkle skittered over to his drawers, finding the perfect one to store it in. Haise and his companions chose that moment to exit the store and step back out into the forest.

While they had obtained an item, they had not found the crux. Their first plan to escape the domain revolved around finding it, and if it could not be located, they would have to fall back on plan B.

As they were returning to the wagon, Haise heard a quiet laugh. It was Mr Binkle. With the door cracked open, he stared at him.

Haise wondered if he had offended him by leaving before offering any polite valediction. He was about to do so when Mr Binkle noted, "He's found you." His laughter continued as he slowly closed the door, eyes shining with that same animalistic glee. "And now he watches you."

# Chapter 6

A cold chill ran down Haise's spine at the thought of someone watching him. Since they'd set off, he hadn't sensed anyone lurking in the forest's shadows or tailing him from a distance. Mr Binkle had closed the door, and the store now shimmered. Its exterior fluttered in and out of sight as though it were glitching out of reality, slipping into the void.

Within a few seconds, the building was replaced by a decrepit old house. The once-hardy beams had given way to a heavy roof and collapsed inwards. Years ago, the windows had shattered, and vines poured through their gaping maws, reaching into the belly of the rotting frame.

The previous owner must have cared for the dead from Helmbi. Once the glowing light from Mr Binkle's store dimmed and fled to the forest, the returning darkness revealed numerous ill-kept gravestones.

The store had been a demonic illusion. The only light now came from the wagon, illuminating Vallas's surprised face.

Haise noticed the wave of qi coming from this trick. *How did I miss that? It should have been obvious.*

Haise worried for the safety of their new parcel and discreetly tucked it away inside his robe's chest pocket. He was adept at losing things and well aware of his clumsiness, although unwilling to admit it. With that in mind, he had considered wearing the necklace. But, without knowing if it possessed the power to cut him into tiny pieces or curse him to never find love, he'd pushed the idea to the side. The last thing Haise needed was a conscious piece of jewellery that detested being worn.

"What the hell! Where'd that weasel go? We didn't even get what we needed! Now what?" Vallas exclaimed, her expression morphing from annoyance to anger and back again. Hiro reclaimed his seat inside the wagon and patted Wulf's head while watching Vallas pace.

"The weasel was not in possession of the crux, yet it was not all for nought. When we escape this domain and reach Norval, we will have an item to trade for information from Akuma," Hiro said as he gave his best smile, but it lacked its usual happiness, and behind its facade blossomed the beginnings of apprehension.

Vallas must have noticed his mood, and she sighed, the aggravation leaving her, replaced by a stern perseverance. Haise hoped her frustration didn't arise from losing her knife.

His chest tightened with remorse for not having relinquished his hairpin.

She clapped Haise's back as if she'd heard his thoughts. "The knife had no significant meaning to me. I'll buy another one in Norval."

"We should try heading towards the forest's centre," said Hiro.

"Are you insane? Why the hell would we want to go there? It's a death sentence," Vallas retorted, her voice flipping back to its previously frustrated tone.

"We have not found the crux, so we should seek the domain holder. They may be in the centre, but they also may not be. We are on the horns of a dilemma, and choosing to move may prove more in our favour than waiting."

She paced while rubbing her forehead. "You can't be serious."

"Are you sure there's no other way?" Haise asked Hiro, who grimly shook his head.

"If there were, I would not have suggested this."

Sighing, Vallas said, "Fine, but the wagon and nimako stay on the main path. We'll go on foot to the centre once we're close enough."

Hiro nodded slightly. "Of course."

The closer you travelled to the centre of a domain, the denser the air became and the harder it was to remain standing, let alone fight. It was where most holders waited patiently for their prey to come to them.

Haise's cultivation level, being intermediate, was far from impressive, but it wasn't the lowest. Thankfully, Hiro was within the transcendent levels, and no doubt Vallas was at the same level or relatively close.

The outcome of any coming battle would ultimately come down to the domain holder's power and experience. The worst situation would be a calamity-level holder, but such a case was highly improbable. There had only ever been a few people to hold this strength. One was the Heavenly Emperor, and the others walked a demonic path. If such an event did come to pass, they would not be leaving alive.

It wouldn't take the nimako long to reach the centre, but Haise's worries had been brewing and he couldn't wait any longer to ask, so he whispered to Hiro, "Is Vallas okay? I don't know her the way you do, but she seems a little frustrated." Haise decided it would be best to downplay the level of her annoyance a bit so as not to appear judgemental.

Hiro's smile was soft, and his eyes were kind as he said, "She was a carefree child, but misfortune befell her family, and bitterness has clung to her ever since." Haise could tell from her wings that she was a child of the spirit-kissed. When Dramour fell to its knees, it had lost its young master and more than half its citizens in the chaos brought forth by the cursed disease. He wouldn't pry into someone's past, especially via another. It was enough to know that Vallas, although crabby, wasn't intentionally lashing out at anyone in particular.

She flicked the reins a couple more times, continuing down the overgrown passage until they reached an area where too many plants lay dying.

"You should remain here, Haise. You are not one for the sword, and your wound is still fresh. I worry . . ." Hiro spoke as if to the winds, his listless words offering his past on a silver platter to something greater than himself and the world, almost in penitence for his inadequacies as a teacher, as a master.

Haise would not be discouraged in the face of truth. After all, he had already been frightened half to death by a crazed weasel. *Can it get much worse?*

"No. I'll be coming with you." He paused momentarily before adding, "I may not have mastered swordplay, and my arm may be a little sore, but I have my lyre. I can still be of use."

Hiro frowned, but Vallas clapped Haise's back and laughed vigourously before she responded.

"Ha! He's got more balls than you." She poked a finger at Hiro as she grinned from ear to ear, bringing an unmistakable flush to Hiro's cheeks.

"All right, all right. Let's get goin'. We're wasting time," Vallas retorted to no one in particular as she enthusiastically sauntered into the forest.

On foot, they ventured off the beaten path, trampling through undergrowth in various states of decay. The putrid mass continued with every step, and branches that could no longer withstand the dense air cracked and fell to the forest floor. The light, which had found it hard to penetrate the canopy, now descended in streams of gold from the heavens, washing over the land as if desperate to cleanse it of the proliferating evil.

Haise was beginning to feel dizzy, and breathing became difficult. "How much further?" he wondered aloud. Wulf had trotted on ahead, but since he was a demon wolf, the miasma this demonic qi created did not affect him.

"We're almost there," Vallas said as her wings flared, allowing her to draw the two short swords from her back. Soon, a howl sounded close by, and as the piercing noise hit the air, twigs around them broke under the weight of several entities. They were surrounded.

They had detected the hostile ploy earlier but walked straight into it instead of avoiding it. Whatever had set this trap, they'd best be ready for an all-out assault. Surprisingly, their host's minions denied them the courtesy of a greeting. With their enemies' approach halted, the trio also came to a stop.

Wulf's snarl tinged the wind with violence. Whatever or whoever it was matched the wolf's sentiment, and their thirst for death became increasingly palpable. Wulf returned to Haise slowly, careful not to spook him and his comrades into drawing their weapons on him instead. The wolf's hackles had risen, and a low growl continued to tumble from his throat as he circled them. He focused on the tree line, and his ears flicked in all directions. More cracking sounded to the right. It was louder, and Haise and his companions each swiftly changed their stance to face the sudden noise.

A collective gasp arose, and Vallas cursed. What pulsated before them stood as tall as the trees, with an aperture large enough to swallow a person whole.

"A rift?" Haise said, his voice tinged with horror, a cold shiver setting his hairs on end. "How did we not sense that? Could our luck get any worse?"

He had seen a rift only once before. Rifts had once been ordinary occurrences before the Heavenly War but had become an incredibly rare sight with the gods' victory. Haise had lost someone to that darkness, and the pain of that memory had scarred his heart and mind alike.

"The domain was strong enough to hide it." Hiro scanned the area around it.

When the realms tore, a gateway between them was called a rift, and the one before them was pulsing with so much demonic qi it had to be connected to the ghost realm. The glow of the rift's shifting edges mimicked a cat's eye as it focused on its prey. At various times, the extremely dark centre would reflect light like a gossamer mirror, the only barrier preventing the two worlds from colliding and collapsing.

In fairy tales, the mirror could take you to a land of wonder where nothing conformed to reality, so all was possible, but this was no fantasy, and on the other side lived the kings of nightmares.

Many of those terrors watched on with bated breath amongst the dying trees as a creature the size and shape of a bear emerged from the surrounding rot. However, its structure was so broken that it could no longer be considered the same. The animal this demon had possessed was long dead and suffering no more, but Haise's heart still ached as it lumbered forth.

Demons possessed lower beings, but few knew of their relentless attacks against the soul. Death to them was simply a means to an end.

Bones cracked as it heaved its way forwards. Unable to cultivate as humans did, they consumed the qi of others. Killing the quickest way, but some preferred to seduce, slowly crippling them.

Wulf huffed as he joined his master's side, as though the demonic wolf had sensed his thoughts and come to remind him that not all demons were like this bear. Wulf had not killed his host. Instead, within him rested two souls, and with Haise's gifted qi, he had become something more. Even Mr Binkle gave the impression of being more than just his race.

The bear twisted to face them, its body bending like a contortionist in a circus act. The display was repulsive, and Haise's stomach knotted as his shaking fingers feathered the lyre, producing a soft mumble of notes.

Given this one's size and aura, it had already managed to kill and devour numerous humans. That and the arrows and sword sticking out of its fur kinda gave it away. Its presence was intense, but it wasn't powerful enough to be a calamity-class being.

The black mass had a muzzle that bared rows of mismatching teeth, and dozens of eyes opened, swirling violently. Its shoulder had been distorted, and chunks of skin hung barely attached. Suddenly, those eyes snapped their focus onto Haise and his companions with a bloodthirsty gaze.

A guttural snarl had thick liquid pouring out of its mouth, pooling amongst the rocks and weeds, which gradually dissolved into a sizzling pile of goop. The smell was foul, so bad that it could be tasted in the air. This was, without doubt, the worst experience Haise's nose had ever encountered.

The bear breathed out, causing Haise's eyes to water and his lungs to burn. To his surprise, he found himself gagging, which just made it even harder to deal with.

"It's fine. I'm fine," Haise murmured. The creature's skin rippled with demonic qi, creating a black aura, and a thick cloud gathered into an even denser miasma at its feet.

"Nope." Haise gagged again, turning around this time. He began to feel bad about offending the demon with his discourteous display. Bodies were bodies, and there were times when they could not be controlled. Hiro had spared a hand to rub his back, but the soothing motion abruptly stopped as Hiro hastily pulled him back.

The world whisked past him as he flew away from the demonic bear, Wulf charging after him. He glimpsed movement. The beast's matted hair shivered across its back as its mangled legs propelled its corpse body forwards. In mere seconds, the earth beneath where Haise had stood was crushed by its enormous weight. With the same speed, Hiro drew his katana and sliced its leg in a clean, fast motion. A sticky residue coated his blade.

The bear's giant maw gaped wide enough to swallow a man whole, and it directed its greedy mouth towards Hiro. With a clang and the scrape of metal on teeth, Vallas redirected the charge to the ground, and Hiro leapt out of the way.

The bear pushed down on its forelimbs. The crunch of bone was audible through its skin as the creature strained against its forward momentum to fling its head back, biting at Vallas.

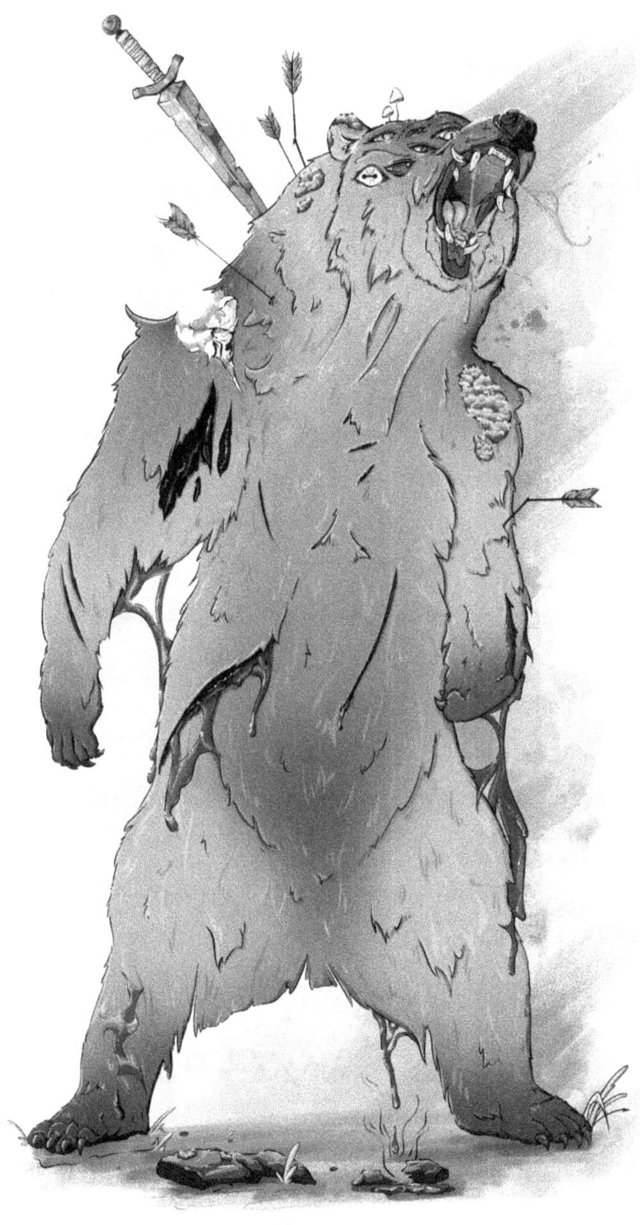

She quickly evaded its mouth by springing herself into the air, using the bear's jerky movements to her advantage and her wings to balance her return to earth.

Haise managed to land on his feet, but the force slid him back against a tree. To his dismay, this tree was less affected by the rot and retained its sturdy disposition. Breath left him at light speed, and an entire galaxy filled his vision. The numerous stars collided into black holes that swallowed his world, turning it black.

Gasping for air, he tried desperately to fill his lungs. They refused to comply with his wishes, as though he were flailing to find the water's surface, trying to overpower the pull of its imaginary hold that slowly dragged him under.

Haise crouched down and applied gentle pressure to his wrist near the base of his thumb. He flooded his blood with a surge of qi to relieve the compressed nerves and building tension in the spasming muscles in his chest.

He drew breath after shaking breath, the harsh air blurring his sight and burning his lungs, as if embers of dying flames suspended in the dense air reignited with the oxygen he consumed. It wasn't his first time experiencing this, and no doubt it wouldn't be the last.

In the time it took him to adjust to the shock, Hiro was at the height of a musical piece, which he played with enough ferocity to push the beast to the ground, its demonic qi wavering under the assault.

Seeing that Haise was all right, Wulf ran back, tearing up leaves that sliced through the air in swirling winds, as though he had summoned hundreds of spiteful nature spirits to wreak havoc and protect the forest. He sank his teeth into one of the bear's legs, and a guttural roar emanated from the vacuous creature. The strength of it sent blood and saliva flying towards them. Hiro blocked it with his arm while Vallas rushed in, taking full advantage of the beast's open mouth.

Haise's wound bled through the white bandage, and in such a state, he was unsure of what he could do to help. He had insisted on coming, and now he was burdening them, a fact that made him resent himself and brought a bitter taste to his tongue. These thoughts faded in the presence of a new occurrence, and shock spread across Haise's features as he heard a man speak.

The familiar, deep-velvet voice whispered from nearby. *Just watching?* What he had heard before upon the mountain was not his imagination but completely real. The pressure exuded by the demonic bear was almost too much to withstand, and the shaking of his breath evolved into full-body tremors.

Splattered with the beast's bodily fluids, Vallas raced past its head and sliced it from maw to tail. Her sharp blade separated flesh from bone with ease. Thick blood oozed down through matted fur, its journey leaving a dark and sticky mess.

She leapt over the bear's back in a way that allowed her to see a full view of the sky, a manoeuvre that positioned her blades perfectly. Her wings balanced her movements as she spun, one rotation after another, causing her blades to cut into the bear's pelt like butter.

Reorienting herself with her wings flared, she landed low and slid backwards with her swords crossed. The attack was over within seconds. The only sign of her passing was the black feathers falling with the leaves; if not for that, one might have assumed their eyes had deceived them. Her skill had Haise staring. He hadn't seen someone fight that well in many years.

The beast ripped around, causing Wulf to release his hold. Its many wrathful eyes swivelled as teeth clamped down right where Vallas had just stood. Dodging back and forth, she avoided all the bear's attempts to strike her.

The unfurling of her crossed swords caused the vile liquid to rain down and stain the soil black. The ringing of metal sang a song of violence, and the smell of iron grew with every onslaught. A crunch of leaves announced her launch towards the target once more, and Wulf followed suit.

Hiro's flute struggled to keep the beast immobile; its effects would not last forever.

Play. Haise.

The sound now came from both deep inside him and behind his ear. It didn't cause him the same dizziness he'd felt on Mount Take. *Was it never the voice that caused it? Should I heed it or dismiss it as a hallucination?*

He glanced over his shoulder and wasn't surprised when no one stood behind him. He turned his attention to the instrument within his grasp, and the ache in his arm grew as he caressed the deep gouge on its fine wooden surface. He felt the phantom brush of cool fingers. Their touch sent goose bumps spreading up his arm and guided his hand to the strings.

"I'm sorry about this," he whispered not to the voice but to the tortured creature that had lost its mind, body, and soul. *I know the pain you feel is far beyond what I could comprehend, so let me release you from what binds you here.*

The scene unfolding before him slowed as he exhaled, and the lyre's beautiful notes filled the demonic space. One after the other, they built a godly melody made for the ravens of death. Even though he missed notes as pain flared through his arm, its shifting tones caused hairs to rise and hearts to quicken.

The bear shuddered, its glare shifted, and Haise was struck by its sheer intensity, as though it possessed the uncanny ability to use unadulterated rage as a form of attack. From its jaws, a low, harsh howl bore down on the music, its strength grappling for control, and the force of it strangled Haise's qi. The resounding result was the unrestricted movement of its limbs, but giving up was never an option for Haise.

He clenched his teeth as the air grew even heavier. He plucked more notes free from their cage as if silently screaming back to the point of a blade; he denied the beast any further say. Using an instrument in combat allowed him to remain at a distance and cause harm to the intangible. The exquisite song ricocheted through the bear's internal organs, doing vastly greater damage to the demon's soul.

He carved his way through the bear to the demon within. His attack was akin to wielding a thousand knives, and Haise's efforts were paying off.

Not done with the foul beast, Hiro played a new piece from *The Poetry of Purification*. The wash of low and slow notes formed a pure melody, which began to disorient the beast and compel it into a state of peace. Haise's music consisted of a higher tonality and easily singled out particular chakra points to destroy the bear's internal connections.

The enemy horde who had encircled them now stormed through nature's debris, dirt, and leaves, forming dust clouds in their wake. Their approach was fast but strange, as stiff limbs caused some to stumble, while others already had missing limbs. Vallas and Wulf turned their attention to what appeared to be the undead, darting to and fro amongst the beings surrounding Haise and Hiro. The battle grew in intensity as they fought tooth and nail to seize victory against this formidable foe and their great numbers.

Bodies fell one after another, and the bear became vacant, its soul almost entirely destroyed. Once no more enemies stood, Vallas instantly switched targets to make a killing blow. Attacking from behind, she plunged her two swords down through the bear's skull. A loud crack, followed by a wet crunch, killed off the music and the beast even more so, its body collapsing into a pile of flesh and fur.

As much as Haise and his arm wished it were over, such a hope was baseless and simply naive. Sealing the rift was essential, and since they were the only ones in the vicinity, the task fell upon their shoulders. If it were left to mushroom, both realms would warp and torment would drench the mortal world, giving birth to a hellscape rivalled only by the Great Heavenly War.

The domain barrier lifted, and golden rays of light streamed across the sky as the sun crawled back to bed. A crisp breeze cleared the smell of blood and rot, but the thickness wasn't entirely alleviated. Haise stumbled closer to the rift. He blinked and shook his head, trying to regain focus.

A short, triumphant bay slipped from Wulf before he returned to the wagon, unable to stay as Hiro's tune changed. Unaware of Haise's predicament, Hiro played a melody that was more elegant and dramatic than those he'd used before. It was the "Song of Ashes" passed down in the Foxx clan, a secret piece renowned for its effectiveness in extracting and erasing demonic energy. Its name stemmed from the blaze ignited by the sound, as any demon within hearing distance would spontaneously combust and the pursuing fire would consume its qi, soul, essence, and flesh, leaving nothing but its bones behind.

A slick sucking emanated from the corpse of the bear as Vallas withdrew her blades. The body seethed with demonic qi, and black liquid the consistency of tar oozed out of every facial orifice. Today the demon's luck had run dry, and the inferno burnt away hair, evaporated qi, and engulfed the beast in a brilliant light. The crackling fire muffled the demon's last hiss of indignation, and the smoke bid the land farewell as it scattered the remains to far corners of the forest.

With the group preoccupied, only Haise peered into the abyss of the rift, and to his mortification, it stared back.

Chapter 7

The silver glow of eyes grew closer as it leisurely approached Haise from the shadows cast across the land beyond, as though it were eternally night. It was a place where no star slept and the moon forever washed the world in a spectral glow. The silhouette was uncanny, the shape becoming more distinct as he drew closer. *It's a person . . .*

There came a sound of chiming metal and the humming of a melody so rich and gentle that it entranced Haise. The sound was so familiar, yet he couldn't remember when or where he'd heard it.

Chains of polished silver with hanging droplets adorned the tops of long boots. They glinted in the light that managed to penetrate the rift's surface.

A person made Haise more nervous than a beast. Humans were less predictable and could easily trap you with their deceit. He was close enough now that the man's lower half was brightened by the warm streams of light. Haise could see only the contours of his upper body, yet those eyes had their own shine that caused the snowy lashes to shimmer.

The whole picture was one of sophistication and regality. The man's thick white hair was tousled by a wind Haise couldn't feel beyond the rift. He was at least a head taller than Haise, with an aura darker than black. It crackled in the space around him as though a brewing electrical storm infused the air with frenetic energy, desperate to explode but forced to obey his every command.

Haise realised his mouth had come open, and embarrassment made his head bow slightly. Soft laughter arose from the silhouette, and more metal whispered when elegant fingers lifted towards the rift, towards Haise. There was a hesitancy in the man's movements, as though his body language carried a complex and subtle meaning he would prefer to keep hidden, but those eyes revealed his tempestuous state.

Given the circumstances, it would have been wise for Haise to withdraw a few steps at least, but something like fear had strangled his heart. His body remained rooted to the spot. Even so, he was curious about who this man was and whether or not it was the rift that had brought him here.

A rogue, bloodthirsty ghost was the worst of all possibilities. They killed without intent, without hesitation, and were the most unpredictable and hellish to defeat.

As the thought occurred to Haise, he could have sworn he saw a smile on the man's face before a single feather floated through the rift. His arm was still bleeding from the impact of being thrown, and the use of his qi via the lyre had made it much worse. Despite that, he raised both arms to protect his face. The movement loosened his bandage, allowing the wetness underneath to grow cold and soothe the burn. Relief flowed through him, and the wash of misplaced pleasure skewed his thoughts.

His attempt at shielding was irrelevant. The feather had missed its mark. Haise followed its lazy path, watching as it gradually came to a stop behind him. Before he could glance back, a radiant light grew around him as thousands of shining white feathers flew past.

Unlike the previous black feather, these were not coated in malevolence, nor did they leak a noxious gas nevertheless, there was something off about them. When they bombarded Haise, he felt no softness, and they had a significant fluff deficiency. *They're not real . . .*

He was scared to study them, remembering what had occurred when he examined the black feather between his thumb and forefinger. He looked down, frozen at the few white feathers clinging to his clothes. It was wafer-thin paper imbued with heavenly qi. He checked for injuries as he brushed them off.

The attack didn't cause any physical damage, nor did he feel any qi draining from him. His soul was not targeted, nor his mind, but confusion seized him. He released a held breath between parted lips. It hadn't missed its mark, because he had never been the target.

The cascade of white mimicked the fall of snow, and the dwindling glimmer of their shine left a glittering scene of remarkable beauty. The qi within those feathers flowed towards the rift, and it began to shrink. His hand lifted unconsciously as though to reach out, but why? What was it that made him want this dangerous figure to stay? Answers . . . maybe?

A feather brushed his hand and slipped between his fingers. Haise pulled it closer. They truly were harmless. He had so many questions flowing through his head as he placed the feather into his satchel.

Who was he? Where had he come from? How had he known the rift was here? Why was the man helping? The need for answers felt more torturous than it should have been, which only made his own actions all the more confusing to him.

The man tilted his head, and Haise could have sworn a smile playfully crossed his face as he turned and dissolved into the darkness beyond. The rift pulled itself together, stitching the dimensions and separating the realms once more.

In the end, what could answers possibly bring him? The man was gone and unlikely to return. With the rift repaired, none of them needed to delve into the demonic realm and make their way alone to Reima, the ruling city within.

Repairing a rift typically required more than one person, one in the demonic realm to use demonic qi, the other in the mortal realm to use heavenly qi. Both acts would consume an extraordinary amount of spiritual energy to heal the rift, so for this stranger to have completed the task from one side and provided enough of both types simultaneously was unfathomable.

Realisation dawned on Haise: The man had used the feathers in place of a person to push the heavenly qi through the tear. Haise should have thanked him. He should have shown his gratitude as best he could.

A feeling of sickness grew within him as his thoughts continued to sink into the marshes of regret. He had assumed the worst, yet his mind, where his morality lay, and his body, where self-preservation persevered, fought each other until they'd built a storm of utter chaos.

That silver stare had glinted with dangerous intent, but Haise had seen in those eyes a more profound emotion that he couldn't explain. The look was less malicious and more voracious. It had entirely stripped him, laying bare his soul, leaving him trapped between the feeling of being preyed upon and the shameful awareness of lost purity.

Breaking through his silent turmoil, Hiro rushed over, having caught sight of Haise lying amidst a sea of dull feathers.

"Are you feeling all right? Can you walk?" Hiro asked as he supported most of Haise's weight and helped him to his feet.

"I can, it's fine. I'm okay, just a little shaken."

"You sure? You're lookin' kinda pale." Vallas spoke matter-of-factly. Sweat had misted Haise's skin at some point, and the dizziness threatened to take him under.

"I've been through worse. I'll be all right after I rest for a little while," he said, speaking as though he were reassuring his companions, but it felt more like he was trying to convince himself.

Hiro accepted his statement, but his lips thinned at Haise's mention of the "little" recuperation time required.

"What's with all the feathers? Did a chicken explode?" Vallas joked to lighten the mood as she supported Haise's other side.

He smiled a little at this, but it faded as he spoke. "There was a person who approached me from within the demonic realm. He sent them through imbued with heavenly qi to close the rift on his own . . ." Haise trailed off, his thoughts a jumbled mess. Hiro seemed surprised that such a feat was possible, which made sense. Haise had never seen or heard of any method close to what he'd witnessed.

"There was only one person? No one else helped him?" Hiro looked understandably confused. Haise wondered if Hiro thought he was delusional and had imagined the entire scene. Or perhaps he assumed Haise had overlooked a second individual, hidden beyond the reaches of his eyes.

"Well, whoever it was saved us a lot of trouble!" This occurrence had assuaged Vallas's worries, and to be honest, Haise also felt relieved. He'd planned to volunteer to venture through the demonic realm, but kindness did not equal helpfulness. His extremely low qi would never come close to the amount needed to close the rift. Even if he had more than enough, Hiro would have used his status as master to stop him. It meant one of the others would have had to leave, and Haise couldn't bear the thought.

"You're right. What's done is done," Haise agreed. They had two other matters to attend to before they continued on their unstable path anyway. Spending time dwelling on this would be a waste. There wasn't enough known about the skill the man had used nor any record of a person who possessed enough power to perform such an act.

This journey was proving to be more than they had bargained for, and Haise had a sinking feeling this was merely the start. His limbs felt leaden as he allowed Hiro and Vallas to guide him towards the remains of their battle.

Along with the missing limbs, he had noticed marks on a couple of the stumbling undead that indicated they had been manipulated by demonic puppeteering. This was a gruesome skill possessed by higher demons to control their victims after death, using their bodies as shields or forcing them into combat.

The bear had been reduced to a pile of bleached bone, as though it had expired in a sea of sand and baked in the arid sun for centuries. The sight was saddening. It had been a while since Haise had witnessed death. He had been numb for too long. He bent to pay his respects to a life lived in horror so that death might bring it peace and beauty, thus allowing its life to regain a tiny portion of its residual meaning.

"Thank you," Haise said. The other two glanced at him queryingly before releasing their hold, allowing him to bend down and examine the human puppets. He was right. Only a few of the victims bore the marks, and they all shared a similar injury. What he had seen were burns, the skin afflicted by flames akin to dragons' breath that seared flesh, tore through muscle, and cooked bone marrow.

A blunt impact had struck their chests, causing several ribs to break, no doubt puncturing lungs and damaging other internal organs, but there was no bruising. After examining the victims further, Haise noted ash in and around all their noses and mouths. It was neither the burns nor the impact that had killed them. It had been asphyxiation that prompted their untimely demise.

He touched his bare finger. He was limited in what he could accomplish here, but he'd still try. Haise could examine each victim's internal qi lines by pouring his own into their bodies. As if the lines were linked to his mind, he could see each structure in its entirety. Any damage to them would indicate physical injury but not show him precisely what was wrong. Following these pathways would lead to the core essence, and damage here would imply that the spirit had been attacked.

Haise could use his qi to examine each victim's internal damage, but he knew he must compromise and check only two: one that had been burnt, and another that appeared entirely unscathed apart from the effects of Vallas's blades and the shrivelled skin and sunken eyes characteristic of complete qi drain.

He gasped in shock as he completed his assessment. Hiro and Vallas peered over him as though expecting to witness a disturbing phenomenon, but neither was privy to the scene unfolding for Haise.

"It's been shattered." Haise pressed his fingers to his lips, as though the simple action might quell the rising fear in his gut, which churned like milk into butter, the solidification creating a weight that hung heavy and burdensome.

"The victim with qi drain has no core essence, as expected. But the individual burnt, struck, and suffocated still has their core essence. It just lies in a thousand pieces. This would have been excruciating." Haise saw Vallas's perplexed face and explained further. "Demons often devour the core essence along with the circulating qi, as it contains the most concentrated amount within the body. A demon would never leave qi behind, not even so much as a hint of its existence. Taking that into consideration along with all the other injuries, it's unlikely that the demonic bear killed these core-shattered victims."

Haise stood to pat down his robe. Trying to improve his appearance was futile. His clothes had been through too much, and only a wash could save them now.

As he ruefully considered this, he also recognised that identifying some of the departed by their clothing might have been possible at one point, but that time had long since passed, making such an endeavour fruitless. The colours had been worn away by weather, different parts were hidden behind coats of dirt and debris, and sections were ripped away or missing entirely.

"Does it matter? Maybe it just wasn't that hungry?" Vallas spoke while rubbing the back of her neck. The fight had caused her some discomfort.

In contrast, the news had set Hiro on edge. Something about one of these victims was causing Haise's mentor some distress. It was unusual, to say the least.

"There have been a couple of cases where demons have not consumed the core essence, not because they were satiated but rather because they were collectors. Instead of using the qi held within, they would display their victims like trophies." Hiro answered Vallas with some hesitation, glancing at Haise as if to gauge his reaction. However, Haise's thoughts were elsewhere.

"It's clear there is another plucking the strings in this macabre dance," Haise muttered as he stumbled off to the wagon.

"We should send a bird to Delfir after getting to Falk. If anyone's seen something like this before, it'll be him. He could help us find out what we're dealing with." Vallas spoke as she followed the two.

She wasn't wrong. If anyone had information about the mortal realm, it would be Delfir.

"Plus, that Dameon is a real smart-arse." She laughed.

"Vallas . . ." Hiro halfheartedly reproached her.

"What? It's true!" she insisted with a grin.

After they returned to the wagon, Haise refused to board and pushed fatigue to the side to walk down the path. The nimako tailed him as he scanned the ground. Haise's collection of autumn blooms spilt over his arms when the stone plaque finally reappeared down the forest path. He placed them carefully around the stone.

The striking difference between the grey rock and the vibrancy of the countless golden flowers made him smile. The deepening pain within him drifted on his sigh. It was hard to know if those who had fallen here would appreciate his presence, but Haise could have sworn he sensed them standing at the tree line. Bowing in thanks, the gathered spirits slowly dispersed to where fate beckoned them. Haise bowed in return, and only then did he board the wagon destined for Norval.

Chapter 8

Night had greedily swallowed the day before the party reached the end of the forest path. They would not reach any town today, as most lay another half day's journey from here. Camping wasn't new to Haise, and the idea of sleeping out in the wilderness had never bothered him as it did most cultivators also blessed by the gods. To live immortal was lonely, and in these hundred or so years, Haise had come to understand why some hid from their grace. Haise himself was never recognised as a fellow cultivator. His behavior lacked sophistication, and he devoted time to tasks regarded as commoners' work. Thus, in the eyes of his peers, he was equivalent to one.

He loved nature. Its beauty was profound, far below surface level, holding incredible knowledge for those with keen enough senses to seek out its hidden treausure. Haise hoped he was one of those lucky enough to have heard its vibrations. He wanted to join its waves of wild song that carried through the mountains and valleys like a giant sky leviathan swimming through the clouds, declaring its eminence.

As Hiro nurtured a fire, Vallas prepped a few makeshift beds. Since only two could fit inside the wagon, Wulf and the third bed's occupant were downgraded to a clear spot near the fire. It took a couple of hours before Hiro's impromptu soup was completed.

Thanks to Delfir's initiative, they were not without food, though Haise wondered why checking for these supplies had slipped his mind. The time he had spent settled in Helmbi had let him relax and notice less, which bothered him.

Whilst travelling as a child with Hiro, Haise had been in charge of supplies and keeping track of the money to buy food and other necessities. He would also chop wood for the coming nights and talk to locals about any recent unnatural disturbances, sometimes asking if they needed help and would be willing to hire him and his sensei.

Hiro had told him it was a kind of training that would prepare him for the harsh realities of life. Haise believed him and gladly took on any work thrown at him. He pushed his body day after day through sickness and pain, but it wasn't until years later that his lessons hit home.

When had he become so lost in the moment? When had his days blurred into one? When had he become so complaisant that he was okay to follow and not act?

He stopped this train of thought; he didn't want to devalue Hiro's meal. Haise cherished the feeling of a fresh breeze, a full belly, and being with those who made a simple place home; such was more than enough to delight one's soul.

There was no wind to chase away the smoke from the campfire, so it continued reaching for the stars as though it longed to embrace its cousins in the sky and drift endlessly. Haise poked the fire with a stick. He gazed into the dancing flames as if expecting the performance of a lifetime to take centre stage.

"You have some friends, Haise." Vallas chuckled and raised a brow with a smirk. Haise dropped the stick when no actors took to the set and drew in a breath at the sight of a new form of light.

They drifted like embers born of fire. Steadily, they fluoresced on and off. Fireflies were in his hair, on his clothes, and flying around in all directions. The insects' ceaseless flashing could hypnotise the absent-minded into a fantasy-filled stupor, their show comparable to the twinkling of fairy wings.

Hiro spoke with great amusement. "They are becoming on you." He did his best to stifle a laugh as Haise gently shooed the tiny creatures back into flight. A boy surrounded by fireflies flickered through his mind. Haise smiled, warmth spreading through him, until his expression faltered.

"You know, it is often said that a deity sends fireflies to let a mortal know they have not been forsaken. That they will watch over them for the rest of eternity," Hiro said in a voice that chased away all doubt, as though he were such an avid reader of folktales that eventually he had grown convinced of their reality and gained the power to imbue others with his own faith. He would make an excellent leader, Haise thought, but he refused the spotlight. He preferred to blend in rather than stand out, to live the life of a humble recluse—not that Haise minded.

"The belief stems from 'The Emperor's Blade,' an old story about a woman and a love that never should have been," Hiro continued. "As a child, the woman was showered with praise and riches, but what she did or said never mattered to her family the way she wished it had.

"Pedestal love demanded perfection, so from the moment she was born, her family turned her into a beautiful porcelain doll, intending her to wed a wealthy bachelor. All their unrealistic expectations weighed too much for her to bear, so each day she prayed for help.

"With a bamboo flute in hand, an impoverished young man living on the outskirts of town came to busk; he alone came to aid her in her time of desperation.

"He hid her away and kept her from the reaching hands of greed. It was only a matter of time before they fell in love, but no sooner had the two understood the feelings they had for each other than the townspeople found her hiding spot. In an attempt to flush them out, they burnt his shack to the ground." Hiro paused as the flames crackled and the wood snapped, unable to resist the pressure of its own weight.

"She died in that fire, her essence smouldering as her core shattered in the heat. The fire spread quickly, and the man saved everyone in its path. He even rescued the perpetrators, which caused a deity to take notice and offer him ascension to the heavenly realm. The woman's ghostly form appeared sometime after. Her devastation was immense. He was her first love, and now he had been taken. Spite bloomed, and she became vindictive. The ground was stained red, and no one in the village remained, but the hole within her only gaped wider. Seeing her anguish and enraged at the shackles around his soul, his body bound to the heavens, all he could do for her was to send a message to tell her that he saw her. That he understood, and that he still loved her. So, day after day, he sent fireflies to dance around her as a show of affection. Eventually, the fireflies expelled her vengeful energy, and once again, he saw that beautiful smile as she moved on, leaving him behind."

The flames flickered and wood cracked again as the fireflies continued their display.

"I'd never heard that story before." Haise was saddened by the tale but also intrigued. Was it truly possible to love another who had fallen so far? More importantly, Hiro had mentioned her core shattering, just like what had happened to some of the victims controlled by the bear. Their wounds were predominantly burns of varying degrees. If heat was the cause of them, it would explain why their cores were so damaged.

"It was Delfir who insisted I listen to his stories. At the time, he told me love was a double-edged sword, and since I owed him, I thought it a reasonable request."

"Well, I wonder who the hell's got their eye on you, Haise." Vallas's laugh was unrestrained. "'Cause by the looks of it . . . they're practically staring!"

Haise chuckled and looked towards the sky, half expecting to see that golden glow once more. All that greeted him was the endless night twinkling with glee as it withheld its many hidden mysteries. Wulf watched as Haise excused himself to seek a quieter place. He ended up near the river they had previously used to wash up in.

He heard Vallas murmur to Hiro, "Was it something I said?"

A huff from Wulf and an equally quiet response from Hiro answered her. "I doubt that. It's been a long day, and we're all tired. I'm sure rest will do us all some good."

The cool air embraced Haise with a silent whisper of acceptance. It did not ask for or expect anything, and Haise felt comfort in its want for nothing, its simple existence. Too many people expected things of those they put far too great a belief in, and too often were they disappointed.

He thought back to Delfir's story of the Ghost King and wondered if his story, too, was wrought with heartbreak. Was it possible he had loved and lost, or was he the perpetrator in his tale of woe? Such was folly for the mind. After all, these were fairy tales spun by mouth and twisted by time.

The peace was short-lived as the same deep voice spoke softly somewhere near and simultaneously from within. *I believe a thank-you is in order.*

His eyes widened, and he became ever so slightly flustered, as if centuries-old butterflies had suddenly decided to hatch and spread their wings. The millions of scales that drifted from their bodies planted fear in Haise's heart.

His caution skyrocketed as he felt for his fan, but it wasn't with him. His mind went blank, at a loss for what to do. "Thank you . . . ?" he responded, painfully aware of how stupid he sounded.

You're welcome.

Haise was dumbfounded. Who in the world was this person, and how could he not sense them? This voice was not his own. There was no way Haise had lost his mind. If that were going to happen, it would have happened long ago. Still, he couldn't pinpoint their position or even make a good guess.

"Where are you? Who are you? What about me could possibly interest you? So much that you saved me from peril and followed me all this way?" He paused, squinting into the night. "Are you stalking me?"

The voice chuckled in response. *To your first question: You ask, and yet you know. As for the rest, I can't say.*

Haise analysed his surroundings again, trying to find anything he might have overlooked.

"They were never attracted to me, I guess . . ." Haise murmured. At those words, the fireflies gathering around the tree next to him dispersed slowly and seemingly reluctantly into the grass.

And here I thought we could chat for a little longer, but that's my cue. There was a large sigh, as though whoever was speaking was disappointed.

"If you didn't want me to know, why encourage me to figure it out?" Haise stepped towards the tree, but they had gone quiet. "Wait!" He faced the fireflies' retreat and reached out, as though he could find the invisible person through touch.

His hand brushed against bark. Its rough texture scratched at Haise's fingers and splintered his hopeful expectations into shards of glass that cut even deeper. He wanted to make them stay, but there was nothing he could think of to achieve that.

Silence fell again over the night, and it seemed the voice would not return. It would be another long day tomorrow, so he returned to camp and slipped into the tent. He knew Hiro worried about his condition and wished he'd stay in the wagon, but Haise sought a new warmth that night. One from flames and fireflies.

Chapter 9

Haise woke to Wulf's fur brushing against his face. At some point, the wolf had made his way into Haise's arms. The heat radiating from him was a blessing, and he took full advantage, since Wulf hardly ever laid this close. He snuggled in further, sucking up his warmth, only to be nudged by Vallas.

"Get up. Time waits for no one. We gotta get goin', so pack up your mat and jump in the back."

He sat up, his hair a complete mess, and somehow his bed was sideways, as though it had tried to escape in the middle of the night. Wulf stared at Haise, his eyes still drooping from sleep. They weren't what you would call early birds. Haise wasn't even sure he wanted to be the second mouse.

They both yawned in sync. Haise reached forwards, stroking the animal's fur, and confirmed what he had thought earlier: It was dull, too dull. The feel of it between his fingers was more like that of a stiff-bristled brush.

"Why didn't you come to me sooner?" Haise probed. Wulf's eyes dropped to Haise's wound, which was still fresh and incredibly painful. It could be that Wulf had sensed his discomfort and that was why he was in Haise's bed this morning.

"You don't need to worry about me so much. You should know by now that I'm a lot stronger than I look," he said as he booped the wolf on the nose. Haise bent forwards, his hands gently pulling Wulf's head down. He kissed his fluffy forehead and allowed his qi to flow into the beast, whose tail waved softly.

"You're welcome." He smiled. Haise was careful when he rose. Although giving Wulf qi didn't knock him out like it used to, it still took a toll. He wavered on his feet momentarily, Wulf letting out a concerned whine. *I'll be fine. I have time to rest . . .*

They hit the road again. On the way to Falk, they would pass through a small village—Hamstead—that was run by a holy woman. The area had never had a leading family, so order couldn't be maintained in the same way it was in other towns, like Helmbi with Lord Delfir and the House of Serpents. This didn't stop the dreams of the few who wished to become cultivators of the arts. People with talents in more combat-based areas often wanted to become soldiers or guards or placed in a role where their skills could shine the brightest.

Since Hamstead had no clan, there weren't any apparent roles for them to play. According to Hiro, many would leave for Norval, a city of endless possibilities. The ones that remained swore their fidelity to the holy priestess and her chosen deities of worship: Rus, the bringer of good harvest, and Felara, the goddess of fertility.

Haise recalled that they weren't all that impressive, but with enough prayer they might be able to send down a blessing or two. Whether that would help the people of Hamstead was up to fate and their collective ingenuity as a community.

The clattering wheels of the cart spoke ill of the old road. The path into town was worn from decades of passage and nature's uncaring hand.

Broken wood was scattered through the grass. It peeked over and around weeds, as if the soil had begun to drag it under where it had fallen. Piles of debris littering the sides of the path caused Haise concern, and it wasn't just him.

After seeing the wooden carcasses, Vallas reined in the nimako, but the damage was already done. The rough terrain was claiming another victim, and the cart buckled with the loss of its front wheel. Everyone braced as it slammed down. Wood splintered and cracked as it bore into the pitted ground. It soon stopped with a heavy thud, as if it were a slain beast taking its final breath. It lay creaking and groaning.

The damage was minimal compared to what had happened to the other vehicles whose remains surrounded them, but Haise could see the pain on Vallas's face as she inspected its condition. The wheel had caught on a shard of wood poking out from a debris pile like a hand reaching desperately for help. It had slipped between the spokes, ripping the entire wheel from its axle and destroying it in the process.

"Why hasn't anyone cleared this area? What the hell are these people doing! You think they'd just . . . just . . ." Vallas was exasperated, her frustration palpable. With a growl, she kicked the culprit, sending it and the wheel flying.

Hiro placed a hand on her shoulder. "You are an incredible craftsman, Vallas. Nothing is ever broken so far that it cannot be mended." Despite his words, Haise could still see the fury in her eyes and the twitching of her clenched jaw. She managed a sigh, clearly trying to focus on less aggravating things.

Haise huffed a little laugh under his breath. In their fight against the bear, she had been so composed, calm, and calculated. Now she had lost it all over the damage done to her cart. Her anger and current inability to focus stood in direct opposition to what he had seen. When faced with this brand-new side of her, Haise couldn't help but feel relieved.

Relieved . . . ? he asked himself. Another person losing their cool was the last thing Haise would have expected to bring him relief. But it was nice to see he wasn't the only one to get mad over silly things . . . though perhaps there was more to it than that.

"Come on. It's not too far on foot to Hamstead from here. Once there, you can ask for some help, while Haise and I will go find rooms for us at an inn." Hiro continued to speak as he guided Vallas away from the wreck. Haise and Wulf followed them down the road to a looming gateway. In the presence of such a gate, the tiny, dilapidated fence extending to either side of it felt quite out of place.

Stones supported its large log columns, which reached high to a carved roof, whose curving slope descended to lanterns that glowed with faux fire. Dusk had come yet again. The small town peeked at its new arrivals, but there were fewer people than Haise had expected.

Hamstead was considered one of the poorer villages in the far-west region, humorously dubbed Deray due to the many past unforeseen tragedies within these mountainous borders. It usually had the bustle of your average town, everyone trying to make ends meet, but today, something was off. Haise just couldn't put his finger on it.

Given Hamstead's size, they weren't likely to have a wainwright or a specialised blacksmith shop like Helmbi or Falk. Even so, it was a farming village, so there should be a general metalworker here at the very least. For intricate work requiring more know-how, the people would turn to the merchants who passed through.

That was fine, since they only needed someone to help them move the carriage, not to repair it. Vallas could handle the repairs herself. After all, she was the designer and builder of this "masterpiece," as she called it.

"I know you said we'd ask someone for help, but . . ." Haise glanced around at the people milling about, and each time he met a person's gaze, their eyes immediately shifted away. He looked down at himself. Appearances aside, there was hardly anything weird about their travelling group.

"Is it just me, or are they all bloody ignoring us? Ugh . . . men," Vallas whispered aggressively.

"Could it be Wulf?" Hiro wondered, redirecting the blow as though it were expected. They all looked at the perplexed demon wolf, and he, in turn, looked back at them. Haise saw only a big, goofy dog, but others wouldn't see him like that, since they hadn't gotten to know him.

"That could be it, but I'm not so sure. They're not giving us a wide berth to avoid Wulf. They're evading eye contact with us. It's as if they don't want to get involved," Haise chipped in as he watched the people pass by.

"Think it has somethin' to do with the destroyed carts?" Vallas added.

"Any work is good work around here. I doubt it's that," Hiro said.

"The priestess may be able to shed some light on this— unless she, too, is inclined to ignore us." Haise mumbled the last part as he looked at Wulf. He didn't want to give the wrong impression, but the idea was not in the realm of impossibility.

"Hmm. A change of plan, then." Hiro frowned, clearly struck by the same concern Haise felt. If the priestess were to ignore them as well and refuse them an audience, it would only prove the existence of a hidden problem they weren't willing to let anyone know about.

Although it would take longer if the weather interfered, it would still be simple enough to leave town and fix the cart where it was. That said, it would hardly be straightforward.

They wandered down the street, past those who hid their gazes under the pretence of work, talk, and play. Thankfully, Hiro knew where the temple was, since he had travelled through Hamstead many times before.

Posted on walls and windows were flyers about a funeral being held today at the temple. A few contained sketched images of the building and surrounding areas. The death of someone was tragic but common, yet it still piqued Haise interest. He pulled a copy down to take with him.

The temple sat perched on a large hill with stairs set into its face. Once they neared the top, the doors conveniently opened, seemingly on their own, and the priestess stood before them as though she'd known they were coming.

"Creepy weirdo . . ." Vallas muttered as the lady, dressed in the purest white with subtle green hues, approached them.

The priestess's eyes narrowed, clearly suspicious of their arrival to the point of almost palpable annoyance.

Unlike the townsfolk, she glared at Wulf in a particular way. Her scorn wasn't a new experience for Haise and certainly not for Wulf. The people from earlier had avoided them all, but she was acting different because of her faith. She stood in reverence to the gods. Being a demon put Wulf in opposition to her beliefs, and Haise's position as protector of said demon put Haise in the same boat. In her eyes, she might as well be looking at two demonic beings rather than one, which didn't bother Haise in the slightest. After all, no one was perfect, and if anyone was demonic here, Haise believed it would be him.

"I saw there was a funeral today. My condolences to the lost and those they left behind. How are you faring these days, Holy Priestess Silvia Farlo?" Hiro elegantly bowed in respect. Having spoken first, he broke the tension between them, allowing Haise a breath as he quickly bowed, mimicking his mentor like he'd done many times before.

"Not well, and the same seems true for you as well. That funeral was held yesterday, not today. Come. Let us speak alone." Her voice was soft like honey but firm, accentuating the point that they were not welcome.

"Of course." Hiro bowed again. "Thank you for allowing me to speak with you." He turned to Haise and Vallas with a questioning look. "Go ahead and find a room at the Bowers Inn. I'll meet back with you later."

Heading back down the hill, Vallas went off on her own. Haise hoped she wouldn't stir up trouble by being too forward. Her spirited nature could come across as rudeness, depending on the person. Haise was fond of her energy, as it gave him more pep, but he could foresee disaster should her tone be taken the wrong way.

"According to the date, we're now a whole day behind in our travels, which means almost two days passed whilst we were trapped within that demonic bear's domain," Haise mumbled to Wulf as he grappled with acceptance. It was no wonder they all felt exhausted after leaving the forest.

"Do you think the locals may be acting this way because of the domain or the destroyed carts? Perhaps it's to do with this recent death? Maybe it was an individual loved by many?" Haise wondered aloud, and Wulf cocked his head. Each person Haise and Wulf passed flicked them glances, but none of them gave any greeting. The whole thing was starting to get a little disturbing. *What is it that makes them act this way?*

There would be no reason for concern if the people always acted like this, but Haise believed they didn't. Hiro would have mentioned something earlier if this were their normal attitude towards strangers.

They made it to the town centre, where a gaudy building proudly announced itself.

Although the Bowers Inn was humble in size, it was clearly trying to make up for that in bizarre appeal. Unlike the houses and stores around the village, it was designed differently, pulling observers' attention and holding it. The owner had spared no expense in making it as unique as possible. However, instead of luxury, it lent itself to the quirky, the novel, and the strange.

It was likely a creation made from the goods merchants had brought in from the south. A traders' paradise lay past Helmbi in the bustling port city called Vale. The town boasted foreign delights that exceeded the expectations of all.

It was a place where *new* was past tense and the future was the present. Where the insatiable went to experience pleasures beyond their wildest dreams and the wealthy spent too much on the twisted. Only the most sought-after and unique things could be found there, and if what you were looking for wasn't at the regular markets, you were likely to find it at the black markets or auction houses.

Rare gems, demonic weapons and poisons, forbidden tomes, exotic meats and pelts, and slaves, be they human, beast, or demon—all that and more could be found there, and the Ramiross family ran it all.

Their group was similar to a clan or house, but not quite the same. Most individuals were unrelated by blood and operated through a chain of command. Unlike other towns, Vale had few rules, and authority was based on power. The head of the family was defined by who the strongest was, and their position could be contested at any time.

Even so, Vale remained a wealthy and prosperous city. Those who had visited said there was nowhere better to find the taste of something exotic and forbidden.

Speaking of Vale . . . Haise remembered Wulf had to use the spatial veil, since he wouldn't be allowed inside the inn. Haise glanced between the door and his companion. By the looks of it, even if he were tolerated inside, he most certainly wouldn't fit.

With a fisted hand at his side, Haise flicked two fingers down, a simple hand signal that resembled an upside-down V, and like magic, Wulf walked into a space Haise couldn't perceive. His coat flowed into a shimmering slip in reality, as though he were consumed by air.

. . .

Haise's room in Bowers was modest, with a fireplace, seating, and a bed. The scent of Vale's exotic spices choked the air, all thanks to not one but four incense burners. It was overkill, the smell was borderline toxic, and even though it had interesting notes, it was far too strong to appreciate. It was as though the innkeepers were trying to mask something beneath it. That wasn't too unusual a concept, but it was still unpleasant to consider.

He bristled at the cold wind pushing through the window as he slid the panel up and locked it. Winter was inching ever closer. They should aim to reach Norval before it struck. Otherwise, the roads around the northern area would be covered in snow and ice.

It would make travelling far more dangerous and take quite a while longer. Either way, they would have to leave the nimako behind. It couldn't withstand the temperatures farther north, so an ox or a couple of draft horses would have to take its place.

Haise peered out to the street below. A couple of men had paused and were in a heated discussion about something Haise couldn't quite make out. Whatever it was, they looked frightened, which was strange. Full-grown men hiding in an alleyway acting paranoid didn't exactly scream *Nothing of interest is happening here, so move along.*

It made him think of Lewis, an old friend who would have been more than willing and far more capable to be nosy in his stead. It had been years since Haise had seen him. He wondered if it wasn't just this moment that made his thoughts wander there but also their next destination: Falk.

The town where he'd lost sight of himself and those around him.

He shook his head and focused harder on the men below, straining to hear their hushed words.

"You don't understand! I . . . can't . . . she . . . help . . . they need . . . med . . . What if it . . . after . . . next?" one of them aggressively whispered.

"Keep her . . . what I . . . do." The other speaker sounded like he was trying to reassure the first. Haise pulled the flyer from his satchel. The one who'd died was Mrs Remmi Lockwood. Though the men's discussion was about a woman, it was unlikely to be her, since she would no longer require "help." But Haise speculated that the two incidents were somehow related and recalled Vallas's comment. *Men.*

When they first arrived, he'd been so preoccupied by the atmosphere and the people's attitude that he hadn't noticed, but almost no women were out and about in the streets as they usually were, shopping and selling.

Had the death of Mrs Lockwood been shocking enough to force all the women into hiding, or was it their husbands keeping them at home to protect them? Even if that was true, that still left their avoidance of Haise and his friends unexplained . . . unless Mrs Lockwood's death was no accident and foul play was involved.

Perhaps the townsfolk were wary of any newcomers because of an unknown threat amongst them—a murderer, still at large. By the way the priestess had been acting earlier, he had to wonder whether it was just Wulf that had spoiled her day. If she needed help, it was likely that Hiro would offer it, even if they were in a hurry or in danger themselves. In Hiro's position, Haise would do the same in a heartbeat.

He didn't stay at the window to watch further, opting to nurse his wound and lie down. Haise was still worried about staying here too long. If Delfir and Hiro were right, whatever had been at the waterfall that day was after him and would no doubt continue to hunt him down. Malevolent beings didn't tend to give up the chase because they were asked nicely.

# Chapter 10

"Yo! Haise!" Vallas barged through his door later in the night, waking Haise from his restless sleep. (Calling it restless was more than it deserved.) She peered down at him like a looming giant, as though she were about to grab him by the ankles and gobble him up.

"Oi. Wake up! I met up with Hiro at the temple after I couldn't find him here. He says he needs your help." Vallas poked him a couple of times as he did his best to right himself. Though his eyes were open, his body felt heavy and stubbornly ignored him. His mind was spinning, trying to comprehend being awake. He was a little baffled. Vallas was here, waking him for help, but if it was as he expected, there was nothing they could do in the middle of the night about a murderer and events they knew little about.

His face clearly expressed his confusion, because Vallas added, "I'm not sure what for, but it might have something to do with the dying lady." She pulled him out of bed by his good arm.

"An injured woman? At the temple?" It might spell disaster for Hamstead if this had anything to do with Mrs Lockwood. A small town such as this would suffer greatly at the hands of a serial killer. Haise immediately left with Vallas, and they walked quickly, Haise doing his best to keep up with Vallas.

"Yeah, a couple of guys brought her in just after sunset. They were begging the priestess to save her," Vallas explained. Haise knew the chances of this being an attempted murder were high. The men had likely saved her life by being there at the right time . . . or were they somehow involved? He knew crossing off any possibility without considering it would not be in their best interest.

They passed the sleeping buildings, their footsteps loud in the quiet night.

"Did Hiro say anything else?" Haise questioned. The woman's current health and connection to Mrs Lockwood's death should have wholly occupied Haise's thoughts. However, he failed to cast aside his aversion to medicinal practice. He loved medicines, poisons, herbs, and the like, but chains shackled this desire while uncertainty stayed his hand. *Will I be of any help?*

"Yeah. The priestess told Hiro the body of Mrs Lockwood was exhumed and stolen. Not only that, but there have been even more deaths since then. I think he said five others have died and the priestess says it's murder!"

They rounded the final turn, and the temple came into view, its stained windows giving off a subtle glow.

"From all the looks, the flyer, and the men in the alley, I had expected something more going on than a single death. I wonder who took her body?" Haise sighed. It could be random, or the killer could have come back for their first victim.

Although Vallas still hadn't articulated what help Haise would provide, she didn't push further when he skirted the unspoken question.

"Men in the alley? You don't seem the type to stalk and eavesdrop," Vallas remarked.

"Well, yes, it wasn't intentional. They just so happened to stop there. I couldn't make out much of what they were discussing, but it did involve a woman, or maybe several, and something about help." Haise paused outside the doors to the temple. Vallas pushed them open and waltzed in while he hesitated at the threshold. If he went inside, he knew he'd have to face a part of him he had long cast aside.

The fear of misfortune crossing his path did not scare him but made him worry for those around him. He wanted to help, but he also didn't want to fail. When he had assisted those who'd been hurt in the past, terrible events had always followed, so he had sworn to himself he would never get involved again.

"Haise?" Hiro called out. He steeled himself the best he could and took that step.

The temple had hundreds of candles lit throughout, filling the ample space with warm light and surrounding him, as though they watched his approach to the two effigies of Rus and Felara. Flashes of staring faces flickered through his mind.

Although the temple was large, it had little seating, as sitting in a temple wasn't considered normal. You would come to give votive offerings, pray, and leave. Vallas took advantage of the few seats available and leaned back into a pew, her ankles crossed on the back of the one in front of her.

She frowned at Haise. "You all good . . . ?" He tensed at her words. She hadn't known Haise for long, yet she still noticed something was up. He sighed, attempting to abate the pounding of his heart.

"Mmm," he managed as he walked up the few steps towards the back of the temple, where Hiro and the priestess stood. She glanced around him as though looking for something. He knew it was Wulf. She wouldn't find him. He wondered if she was pleased by his demon's absence or suspicious of its whereabouts.

On top of a makeshift bed of blankets, the lady lay on her back. He saw several bruises and minor cuts as he rolled her onto her side. He checked the flow of her qi, the presence of her core, the level of her consciousness, the state of her clothing and any other incongruencies.

"Miss. Can you tell me your name?" Haise examined her back as she responded.

"Penelope." Her voice was quiet and quivering.

"How old are you, Penelope?" Haise kept her talking while he finished checking her eyes. Her face was covered in blood, so it was hard to see any minor injuries, but in the face of what Haise was seeing, a few cuts were low on his list of worries.

One of her eyes was missing. There was a lot of swelling, so it was hard to tell what condition the other was in. To think someone was capable of committing an act so aggressive was beyond unsettling.

"Thirty-four. Please, it hurts so much," she pleaded softly.

"I understand. I'm here to . . . help. I'll ease your pain," Haise answered gently as he rested back into seiza, a position that made placing the lyre on his thighs easier. Still tender from the fight, he held it delicately as his fingers brushed the strings.

When imbued with heavenly qi, several pieces of music could significantly reduce pain, but they would offer nothing by way of actual healing. He had spent many years studying songs, reading tome after tome, and writing to explore various benefits. His relentless effort had become borderline obsession as he searched and studied the rarest pieces, including those with multiple effects.

It was by far most common for a song to contain only one ability when played to its fullest. Now and then, pieces were created that held the capacity to affect more than one aspect. The last song from *Purification VI* boasted this power.

Slow and soft notes echoed throughout the temple hall as Haise lightly plucked the strings and brushed his fingertips across Akin. The vibrations melded with his heavenly qi to produce a mellow and whimsical melody.

Her pained face eased as his music continued until its last note, the space falling silent again. The song would not work on him, as the player could never be affected by their own music. He could ask Hiro to play something for him, but his pain was a helpful reminder of his fate.

The candles flickered, and he felt watched by the shadows, their faces flashing into his mind once more to continue their judgement, as though they waited with bated breath for him to make even a trivial mistake.

With a sigh, Penelope seemed to fall asleep, and Haise took that moment to escape the shrinking room. He was starting to find it hard to breathe. Self-doubt materialised, resting on his back and dragging his will to the gutter. Walking out onto the steps before the temple was the only way to gain relief. As he did so, the weight lifted off his shoulders.

Hiro touched his shoulder. "I'm sorry, Haise. I should have known this would affect you the way it has." He paused, but Haise said nothing. What was there to say? He knew Hiro meant what he said, but that didn't make it any better. His emotions and ideals warred against each other.

Helping people was something Haise aimed to do in every aspect, and he had done so since he was a child. However, it still brought back those unwanted memories.

"You don't have to help anymore, Haise. How about you stay at the inn until we're done? Vallas will come and get you when she's managed to repair the cart." Hiro did his best to reassure Haise that leaving would be completely fine, but it wouldn't ease the spreading guilt in his chest.

Haise left without a word. He found it too hard to look at his master, for if Hiro looked too closely, he would see him for the coward he was. All he wanted was to be of use to someone, to be good enough, to be worthy of praise. No matter how hard he worked day after day, it never got any easier to accept the truth.

He would always be broken.

# Chapter 11

The inn was as still as the night, its structure neither creaking nor groaning in the wind. Haise sipped the tea he had brought to his room. Surprisingly, the inn offered night services, which most likely correlated with the guests they usually received. Merchants wouldn't always arrive during the day, but they still needed places to stay and warm food to eat. It was almost mandatory for good business to serve them.

He sat in the eerie silence, wondering if he had done the right thing. With no clan and only a small group of cultivators in the area, figuring out what was happening would take some time. With Hiro added to their ranks, it would be easier, yet he sat here doing nothing because of . . . what? Events in the past shouldn't control him in the present, so why did he feel their claws so deep within his body?

Back and forth, he went from sleeping restlessly to sipping tea until he could take the self-induced torment no longer. Enough was enough. He might have difficulty helping the injured, but nothing was stopping him from investigating the scenes where these acts were committed.

Haise used a piece of complimentary paper to write a quick note about what he planned to do in case Vallas or Hiro came looking for him. He left the inn in a huff, determined to do something. That is, until he realised he was lost and had never had a destination to begin with.

He glanced around at the few people opening stores as the sun rose, rays filtering through house windows and glinting off metallic surfaces. They still turned their eyes away from Haise even before Wulf emerged from the veil to walk beside him.

Again, he noticed almost no women. These murders must terrify them enough that they'd put themselves in hiding, or else those who cared for them had. Haise wasn't surprised. If it were him and he had someone dear to him in that way, he too would do his best to protect them.

Rounding one bend after another, Haise thought he would eventually find somewhere he recognised, but he'd given Hamstead little credit. Although small on a map, it wasn't in reality.

Deciding to go left or right once more, Haise caught a smell all too familiar, and his face paled. Off the beaten road down a long alley lay the body of a deceased woman. Her sickly green skin slipped in various places as maggots seethed where her eyes used to be.

Haise brought a sleeve to his nose and bent to look closer around her eye sockets. He wanted to confirm a hunch that had arisen when he helped Penelope in the temple. It was just as he thought. Blood clotting and inflammation surrounded the injured areas, and dried, discoloured blood pooled underneath her upper body. She had been alive as her eyes were gouged from her face, but why do such a thing? Haise needed to know more about the victims to understand the killer.

Placing two fingers against her wrist, Haise sent qi throughout her body, investigating the current structure of her qi lines, and found no obvious damage. Decomposition put her at roughly two days. Apart from what you would usually expect, only one thing stood out as strange to Haise: Her core had been marginally cracked.

There had been some kind of struggle or pressure on her spirit. It was likely this strain, with the added blood loss, that had caused her death. Whoever the killer was, they were no novice. They undoubtedly had a talent based within the arts of spirituality, which was rare but not unheard of. Even Haise's talent, healing sound, could be considered a spiritual talent due to its possibility of interacting with the soul.

Wulf was sniffing the areas surrounding the body, a behaviour Haise hadn't seen in a while.

"Wulf?" He walked over to peek at what the demon found so fascinating. With a snort, Wulf trotted down the alley, and with seconds to decide whether to stay with the body or follow, Haise blew caution to the wind.

The worry he felt about others stumbling across the woman was temporary. No one had found her yet, since this part of town was more ghost than person, and he had a feeling Wulf was headed somewhere more important. He pulled off his outer robe and flicked it over the victim, hiding her body from immediate view.

The further Wulf took him, the more the town changed. The buildings were increasingly run-down with every passing step, each seeming more abandoned than the last. Windows were boarded, and rubbish decorated the nooks. The contrast to the well-maintained shopping district in the middle of town was stark. It was as if they had stepped into another world.

Finally, the wolf stopped at the front of a dilapidated house and looked questioningly towards Haise.

"What?" When Wulf brought a paw to the door, Haise glanced between him and the house.

"It looks fairly abandoned, Wulf." Haise knocked, and when there was no response, he went around to the back. There had been a fence at one point, though what remained was barely a ghost of its former self. They both peeked through the back door and saw little to no furniture, dust-covered surfaces, and—

"Ahh!" Haise stumbled back as quick-moving shapes darted from the door's broken panels. Wulf snatch one up, raising his tail and puffing out his fluffy chest.

"Ah . . . thanks." Haise chuckled and patted the wolf's head as he examined his catch. It was a dust devil—one of the little creatures born from dense residual demonic qi adhering to random objects. The items absorbed the qi, morphing it into these tiny beings. They were, for the most part, harmless, but they did tend to steal small shiny things and were notoriously mischievous.

It wasn't dust devils or residual demonic qi that Haise was interested in; it was why they were here in the first place. The evidence before him was simply the symptoms of a past event, though figuring out which one might not be possible.

The door was left unlocked, so Haise stepped in to nose around a little, though out of everything he was expecting to find, it wasn't a ritual circle.

The air was stale with old smoke and dust. Upon the floor, painted in blood, were markings for summoning a demon. Burnt-out candles staggered about the circle, wax pooling around each one and running to the centre of the bloody symbol.

"Is this what you sensed, Wulf?" The demon wolf gave him a knowing expression and huffed as though it were obvious and the question was stupid. The blood was dried and flaking. Between this, the melted candles, and the accumulated dust, it looked as if the house had been vacant for at least a month.

"Do you think this has something to do with the murders, Wulf?"

"Possibly." The unexpected response had Haise spinning and drawing his bladed fan. Hiro fumbled, his usual elegance replaced with remorse for frightening Haise. He patted Haise's head lightly, clearly unsure what else to do.

"Sorry, Haise. I didn't mean to scare you. Vallas, a few other cultivators, and I found three more bodies in the slums. I spoke to the priestess, and the number of people going missing or being found dead has more than doubled recently. I asked if there was anything odd or uncommon that happened before any of these deaths, and she mentioned a child who had an accident. Her mother was Mrs Lockwood, and they lived here. Apart from that, there had been no other suspicious deaths." Hiro spoke solemnly.

Haise closed his fan. "I also found a body. Were the three that you found all women?"

"No. One of them was a man, which I found alarming. It was starting to look as though our serial killer preferred women." Hiro paused, stress evident across his features. "And I still believe that to be true."

"You think there are two?"

"Possibly. The injuries to the man were . . . different." Hiro frowned, deep in thought.

"Different how?"

"His eyes were still intact, for starters. I'm not an expert like you, Haise. However, he looked a lot like the few burnt victims in the forest. It was as if he had been in a house fire."

"That's . . ." Haise didn't know how to finish. *Impossible . . . strange . . . concerning.*

Mentally setting the women aside and focusing on the burnt victims, he felt as though they had been deliberately killed as some form of message. *To whom?* he wondered, praying the message wasn't meant for them. But prayer wouldn't save them from the probable truth.

They had found those bodies. Sure, another could have discovered them first, but it would have to have been very recent, considering the timing of the victims' deaths. Conjecture would get him nowhere, but the thought was terrifying.

"This has been too easy." Hiro was staring at the circle of candles. He was right. They were conveniently finding bodies that took no effort to hide their stories.

"If our killer is a demon, then I'm not surprised." Hiro left with Wulf as Haise continued to gaze at the bloody ancient symbols.

"A demon-summoning ritual? How strange. Perhaps there's more to the child's death, as the priestess suggested. What were your terms, demon . . . ?" Haise mumbled to himself.

Such a ritual drew a contract between the summoner and a demon, the terms of which stipulated that a task the summoner requested must be completed before the demon could have their body. It was a contract of self-sacrifice, where the most common demand was gruesome revenge.

If the request was to kill someone and they died by disease, for example, the task would be considered not accomplished. Having not successfully achieved the terms of the summoning contract, the demon would be pulled back into the demonic realm, but the summoner would still lose their life.

To go to such lengths, whoever did this had been desperate and unable to find a better way . . . or they didn't want to. Like Hiro said, there was more here than met the eye, and with luck, it might lead to Hamstead's elusive killer.

If there *was* more to this and a demon was involved, they would have to be careful. Haise didn't want to go up against a humanoid demon, the most dangerous of their kind.

Finally, he too left the enigma behind and squinted as he emerged from the house into the full force of morning rays. The light pursued the shadows relentlessly, and within them, Haise noticed lots of movement. Tiny darting shapes paused to hide under stairs, peek through windows, and peer from trees. Haise caught up to Hiro and Wulf and explained where he and the wolf had found the body as more dust devils followed in their wake.

There were hundreds. This explained the cart issue and the graveyard of wood they had seen. The dust devils had no doubt succumbed to their primal urge to steal. With missing bolts and similar fixtures, the carts stood no chance against the worn roads.

"There are too many," Haise said, scanning the cracks and recesses they tucked themselves into.

"I know," Hiro agreed, doing the same. Half as many could easily have been explained by the completion of one demonic ritual. A few more would suggest the death of a powerful individual, their body leaking demonic qi. The only thing that could produce this many was the remanence of a rift.

"A man bearing the same injuries we saw around the bear . . . and another rift." Saying it aloud didn't help Haise come to terms with the knowledge as he'd hoped.

"I'll have a few of the local cultivators bring the body of the woman you found to the temple. For now, I think it might be best for you to return to the inn."

"I'll be fine, plus I need to examine the man myself." Haise was grateful for Hiro's consideration, but hiding from this only made it worse. His internal monologue recited his morals and battled his trepidation.

It wasn't hard to tell which won. Haise knew these victims and their families needed help. He had the means to achieve results, even if he found it challenging.

"All right. But Haise, please don't push yourself." Hiro gave him a warm smile as they reached the steps to the temple. Haise wished the walk had taken longer. He entered again, this time looking down as he drew closer to the statues of the gods.

The woman who had survived her encounter with the killer was no longer here, and in her stead were four bodies. Coldness licked the corners of his eyes, faces still lurking and sneering around him.

He did his best to focus on the bodies before him, pulling down the white cloths that offered respect to reveal the faces of three women and one man. All the women shared similar injuries: gouged eyes, bodies slightly sunken skin from qi drain, cuts and scrapes from a struggle.

The man, however, did indeed resemble the burnt victims in the forest. His skin was black, with bone showing in various places; he had blunt-force trauma to his chest and smoke inside his nose and mouth. Whatever had slain this man was the same force that had ended the lives of those burnt in the forest and, by all appearances, separate from the Hamstead Killer.

Haise checked the man's core and confirmed it was also shattered, as though it were hot glass that had cooled too rapidly. He was about to stand up when a curl of demonic qi caught his eye, and what lay there was shocking. Haise gently touched the victim's injured arm as he stared at the feather half embedded in the man's skin.

"Who moved this body? Was anyone hurt?" Haise looked up, frightened of what this could mean. Glancing around, Haise realised it was only him and Hiro. He had been so careful not to look around that he hadn't noticed they were alone.

Hiro took it in stride and answered him, leaving his embarrassment to melt away. "No one was wounded. Why? Is something amiss?"

"The black feather. The same kind from the mountain that caused my injury. One is stuck in this man's body." Suddenly, the burns made sense. While Haise hadn't searched the whole forest, what they had seen showed no sign of a large fire.

"There was no burnt-down structure where they found this man, was there?" Haise ventured.

"No, but a small trail of burn marks was nearby. They were similar to footprints but not human. Even without the priestess giving me the address to the child's home, the prints would have led me to the house."

"The demonic feather, burnt victims, the trail, and, of course, the rifts. They're all connected, and what we're seeing now is the aftermath of their path to me." After replacing the white cloth on each victim, Haise cautiously stepped back.

He was extra careful with the man, as though the feather would dislodge itself at any moment and become part of him, burning its way through him until nothing remained.

Chills ran down his spine as nausea threatened to rear its ugly head. Haise was reminded of his fate. To be feared was to be hunted; at least, that was why most beings like him were killed.

The fault was his alone. He had done so many things wrong. Perhaps the maw of this beast was to be his end, yet something pushed him forwards. He didn't fear dying . . . or maybe he did.

"I'll tell the others to be careful when moving the bodies. Haise, are you feeling okay? Is there anything I can do to help?" Hiro placed a hand on Haise's back and guided him out of the temple.

"Yeah, I'm fine. We need to bring this killer into the light and leave. I don't want it to find me here and get more innocent people involved." Although he was frightened of the possible outcome, he refused to rush anything. The more flustered one became, the more one missed—a recent lesson he'd learnt from Hiro that would forever control his actions.

Chapter 12

The sound of music escaped the inn, whispering of secret adventures and dangerous beasts, of wonder and the awe of magic. People sat and stood around, listening to a man sing about myths and mystery. His troupe backed him up perfectly with shifting notes to match his story and tone, bringing out the best in their instruments as together they wove tales both old and new.

Haise and Hiro joined the crowd as a new story began, one about a horse and its ghostly horror.

". . . Flakes of gold rise as they fall into flame / Stalking, it follows the steps of fellows / Burning from the inside out / Hunting in the shadows of night / Smouldering violence, a ghost of defiance / Is the black horse . . . the black horse of death!" He sang with gusto, his energy stealing and holding the attention of everyone in the audience—all except one.

"This isn't just a tale, you know. The horse is real. I've seen it," spoke a tiny voice at Haise's side. It sounded like a child, although he couldn't tell who said it.

Even though the music and drink were drawing in more and more people wanting a release from the rising stress and tension caused by recent events, there were still plenty of suspicious looks directed towards Haise and his companions, and still there were hardly any women amongst those assembled.

The crowd had suprisingly grown to a point where new arrivals who wanted to listen in had to do so from outside.

Vallas had also rocked up. She and Hiro were speaking to one another across the room, and Wulf had sneaked out of the veil behind her. It was said that using the veil wasn't difficult for those who could, but it still appeared draining to keep oneself within its space for long periods.

There should be no children out at a time like this, but Haise saw a few, guarded closely by their fathers. They were laughing and clapping to the music, innocent to the dangers of the world around them. However, none were close enough for him to hear them clearly. He didn't want to assume he was mistaken, as he'd been before, seeing how his presumptions had been entirely wrong when it came to the voice in his head. Dread washed over him. *You're not another voice, are you . . . ?*

Haise's thoughts huffed aggressively at him. He pinched his nose, exasperated at how insane he was starting to feel and sound. A hand slipped down his face as the little voice giggled. "Wanna play hide-and-seek? If you wanna know about the horse, you better play with me! Find me if you can!"

Generally speaking, any information was good, and Haise knew very little about his would-be assassin. He should be willing to do just about anything to get it. However, Haise was not that great at hide-and-seek, *not great* being the understatement of the year. When he'd played as a child, he was always found first, and gods help his friends if he was the seeker.

Wulf had pricked his ears, alert to Haise's frustration. Haise signalled for the wolf to stay. The last thing they needed was a mass of fur and slobber scaring the crap out of everyone here as it eagerly pushed through the crowd towards Haise.

He knew it would be safer if Wulf came, but he couldn't wait, and nothing would come of this if he didn't try, so he quickly left the inn to wander the streets. Haise searched every place that seemed capable of concealing someone, poking his head into little hiding places and nosing around bushes. The day dwindled until dusk set the lanterns ablaze and the night crept into place.

He had just sighed, almost ready to give up, when he saw a little girl around the old dust devil–infested houses in the slums. She sat on the stairs across from the home hosting the demon-summoning circle, legs flicking back and forth. Impatience had most certainly saved her from hours of hiding, as though some god had found enough mercy towards him to let her know just how terrible he was at this.

"Sorry. I started to feel bad for you." She smiled at Haise, pity lacing her expression. "Have you never played hide-and-seek before?" Her question was so pure and innocent Haise didn't know whether to cry or laugh. He was simultaneously struck with both embarrassment and complete acceptance of his subpar skill in the children's game.

"Why here?" he curiously poked while closing the gap between them. Light passed through her silhouette. A shadow was missing where there should have been one, and there was a faint transparency to her. She was a skinless ghost.

"'Cause that's my home. I like coming home, but Mummy doesn't love me anymore. She cries every time she sees me, so I stay away to make her happy." She paused, kicking her legs around so that she faced Haise as he sat down next to her. He rubbed at his ankle, the old wound giving him grief.

"Wouldn't you do anything to make your mummy happy?" She spoke again with innocent eyes, as though naive to the world's harshness yet still tainted by its brutality.

"Of course I would, but your mother still loves you. She just isn't showing it in the same way anymore." Haise couldn't know whether or not that was true, but the validity of his words was not their purpose. He remembered how kind his mother was, how often he would grow ill and how she would care for him even if she was sick herself.

Haise did his best to approach the topic cautiously and with as much consideration as possible. "Did you ever have any fights with your mother? I know I had a few," Haise ventured. It wasn't uncommon for the dead to forget how they'd died. Not only that, but they also tended to hide their deceased appearance. If he could get a handle on the child's relationship with her mother, it might shine more light on the circumstances of her death.

It could also help explain why there was evidence of a demon-summoning ritual in her house. He didn't want to assume, but it was starting to look more and more like Mrs Lockwood was the killer—or, rather, the demon now possessing her dead body was.

If he knew for certain, perhaps it could give the families who had lost loved ones some form of closure.

"No, but Mummy was always angry at our neighbours. She didn't like the way their kids used to play with me." She jumped up, and Haise followed suit, unwilling to let her out of his sight.

"Did they play hide-and-seek with you?" Haise watched attentively for any reaction his words might provoke. She started skipping down the street, farther into the slums and towards the edge of town.

"No, that's my favourite game. They didn't wanna play that. They liked truth or dare." She paused at the side of the River Spry. Running from the mountains of Dramour through

Falk, into Hamstead, past Helmbi, and out to sea near Vale, the Spry was the oldest river that had survived the Heavenly War with little change in its path.

"Did they make you do things you didn't want to do? Is that why your mother was angry?"

Her lips pursed, and she hovered on the verge of tears. He had hit a nerve, and his panic prevented the oh-so-helpful art of speech.

"It's all their fault! I told them I couldn't swim, and they still pushed me! Now Mummy's mad, and she won't listen to me, because I can't swim. I just wanted her to be proud of me . . ." She mumbled the last part, referencing a feeling he knew all too well.

At this, her appearance changed. Wet clothes clung to her pale, translucent body, but one detail in particular stood out to Haise. She was blind. The hollowness to her gaze was not an exaggeration; she had been born with no sight.

His expression softened. He would hug her if he could. Instead, Haise bent down and smiled. "She's not mad at you. If anything, she is so proud she doesn't know how to tell you."

"You can't know that." The girl was defiant and suspicious, which Haise had expected, but that wouldn't stop him from trying to ease her mind and heart.

"Of course I can! I am a god, after all, but you'll have to keep that a secret, okay?" he whispered. At this, her eyes lit up, and she nodded vigorously. Haise was glad he could make her feel better. But they had a bigger problem now, and it was getting closer by the second.

"If you tell me a little about the black horse, we could play another game of hide-and-seek. Maybe you could help me get better at it?" Haise smiled, and she took the bait.

"Yes! The black horse is called Kuro, and he's looking for his other half!" she yelled. Death having released her from blindness, she dashed off to find the best hiding spot he would never discover.

Though he had hoped for more information, it was for the best. A dark aura had gathered a few houses away. Slowly, he turned to face what had come to sniff him out, hoping it wasn't the black horse of death, Kuro.

# Chapter 13

Closing the distance was not a horse. Instead, it was a somewhat dishevelled woman possessed by none other than our resident demon.

"No longer hiding in the shadows? At least that makes this easier," Haise mumbled to himself.

The incomplete possession made Mrs Lockwood's stare vacant. Eyes were passages to the soul, and hers was trapped under layers of demonic manipulation. A smile of twisted pleasure spread across her face.

"Mrs Lockwood," Haise called out.

She giggled. Her voice was warped and wrong. "What did she ask you to do?" Haise narrowed his eyes, his tone surprisingly aggressive. He knew the woman was already dead, yet that knowledge didn't make this any easier.

She chuckled. "Poor little soul. Lost your way? You'll never find him!" She lunged, and the distance closed so quickly that Haise barely had time to react. She struck at his head without hesitation, and he did his best to avoid the full impact.

Haise's nose and lip stung, and although he managed to evade the fatal blow, blood trickled down his face. He steadied himself while he considered her words. Was she referring to Kuro . . . or perhaps Akuma, the demon king?

"I'll never find who?"

She grinned ear to ear, as if pleased by Haise's interest.

"She wanted revenge for her daughter's suffering"—she laughed as she drew closer to Haise again—"all because she can't see!" The demon mocked Mrs Lockwood. *"It's not her fault! Take their eyes! Make their mothers suffer for not raising them right!"* She hissed and came at him again.

Haise was ready to counter her attack this time, so he reached out once she was close enough. All it took was one finger, the right spot, and a small amount of qi. He sent waves of vibrations through her, mimicking "Ballad of Death." Unlike "Song of Rest," this one was played against the unwilling and held some resemblance to the one he'd used while fighting the bear.

The demon reeled backwards in pain from the sudden internal onslaught. Her shock was replaced by glee no sooner than it had appeared. Blood ran down from every orifice, as though her body had felt the force of an explosion or a blood arts talent had been used to drain her of every drop.

"Your display, the way you kill them. Why make it easier for us to hunt you?" Haise huffed, his heart racing.

She smiled as if enjoying every moment of violence, but Haise knew he had damaged her vessel significantly.

"The more I kill, the stronger I become, and what's better than stupid cultivators with so much qi but no idea how to use it?" She laughed maniacally as she went to attack again, but she was much slower.

Haise touched the blood dripping from his nose and brushed it down the outside of his fan. He flicked it open, each blade glinting and pristine, their edges honed with such care that each could slice through stone. He closed his eyes, focusing on the blood, which dissolved into the fan.

Everything stilled, the tension in the air growing as the blades grew hot. The surface rippled as it shifted colours from white to a dull red, as though the blood churned in darkness and tainted its pure core. What he was trying to pull off required quite a bit of demonic qi, which he didn't have. Sacrificing more than he could offer would take a tremendous toll on his body. Still, it was better than dying here.

The space around Haise shivered as the catalyst absorbed his demonic qi. The demon ran at him, screaming as she pounced. He parried her movement easily, turning in time to use the opening she had created. In an instant, he released the blades from the fan with a strong sweep. The motion aggravated his wound, causing him to flinch and withhold some of his strength.

A few blades missed the mark, the rest embedding themselves in her back. It was a small victory, but Haise would take it. The demonic qi acted like a poison. Thick black snaking lines crawled under her skin from the wound as though a wicked curse had taken hold, damning the demon's soul to eternal suffering, as she had done to the others.

Anger split her face into an expression devoid of humour. She was done smiling. Each consecutive scream sounded less and less human as she rushed him again. The poison was doing its job, and the demon would eventually succumb to its potency.

Haise was at the end of his strength, his energy taken by the spell upon his blades. The demon wouldn't die in time, so he had to escape, and do it quickly. Hiro wouldn't be coming to save him this time, and he'd stupidly told Wulf to stay. None of the others knew where he was, and even if they did, Haise doubted they could get here in time.

He moved down a narrow path towards the outskirts of town, drawing the demon away from the townsfolk, knowing he was further isolating himself from help. To his dismay, the path ended at a wall. The cruelty of it all was ironic. Wishing for escape and receiving a wall perfectly explained his luck in life.

He faced the demon one last time as her smile returned, displaying her immense pleasure, her evident satisfaction in having trapped her prey. She teased Haise step by step, yet he sensed a note of reluctance, as though she were increasingly afraid of something.

There were only a few more steps he could take backwards before he hit the wall, yet a strange feeling of warmth grew behind Haise as energy gathered around him. She leant forwards as though to leap and close the distance, but instead she shuddered, as though the air had turned sour and bitterly cold.

"My Lo . . ." She choked as though an invisible rope had caught around her throat and tightened.

Haise felt that same sudden coolness. It brushed his back, goose bumps spreading across his body like waves. Darkness pooled around his feet, tumbling towards the demon. Akin to fog, it rolled into the light which struggled to penetrate its surface no matter its persistence.

The demonic qi surrounding him now was far thicker than what the bear exuded, and yet Haise didn't feel sick, as if the qi were somehow his own, flowing playfully around his robe.

The presence behind him was immense. There were no words for the pressure it exuded. Scratching at her neck, the demon continued to take several paces back, away from whatever was now behind Haise. The murderous intent oozing off this being was palpable, yet Haise didn't feel in danger. In fact, he felt oddly safer, which concerned him. He should be evading both hostile entities, not cosying up to one.

The whisper of metal and the brush of fabric were loud in the growing tension as a hand reached around his waist, pulling him back. There was an apparent strength to who held him, but there was also a gentleness to their movements, as though they were tentative or averse to harming him further.

"Haise," they murmured softly, their deep voice holding notes of tension and overwhelming anger. Haise must have heard them wrong. After all, he could count on one hand how many people knew his name. Even so, a part of him kept saying he knew this voice. The echoes of past words flittered through his racing mind.

The voice held the same notes of warmth and roughness he remembered. Haise was lost in the realisation when the person's other hand rose past his head, long fingers reaching towards the retreating demon. The elegant motion lacked fear, as though they were simply reaching for an item.

"Now we play by my rules." The voice dripped with animosity.

The air crackled with power as ripples turned to vast amounts of dense, roiling demonic qi raining down from their hand. The black energy glittered as it spun itself together, each cloud taking form, all of them joining like pieces of a puzzle, destined to become something more than what they were created to be.

The settling mass locked on to the fleeing demon as she turned and clambered for escape. In a fraction of a moment, the creation surged forwards. Its body rolled and writhed as it threw itself down the alley, pieces of debris crumbling as it made impact.

A piercing scream of pain crawled from the demon's throat, ripping its way out of her mouth, as the creature's glistening teeth crushed her bones with disturbing ease. The creature propelled its snakelike body to the skies as though it were a heavenly beast aged by time, changed by hate, and possessed by instinct.

Scales of dazzling black reflected specks of colour as silver eyes shone brightly through the mass of darkness. Haise had almost forgotten the hand around his waist until it tightened, bringing him against the figure. He stilled, unsure of what they intended to do next, but to his surprise, more qi collected in his saviour's hand as it formed a parasol.

It rose over Haise's head just as the sound of droplets hit. Splatters of blood blossomed on the stone path and ran down the walls around them. The sight and sound made Haise reel, even though he knew Mrs Lockwood was no longer alive. The noises he had heard came only from the demon controlling her body. Memories and emotions he had hoped would stay buried rose to the surface.

Slender fingers reached into his chest pocket and retrieved the pendant he'd gotten from Mr Binkle.

"So, you do have it." The voice was so heavy and close that Haise felt the need to move forwards, but he couldn't.

The chain unfurled as they used qi to clip the necklace around Haise's neck, their fingers brushing the stone and stalling his mind. The jewel shone brilliantly under their gentle touch. Foreign qi entwined with his own, mixing and overflowing like a glass of wine unable to contain the flow of sweet liquid. Haise grew hot from its invasion, reflexively gripping the fan and its remaining blade tighter.

He was convinced: This was the physical form of the voice he'd been hearing, and they had slipped out of the veil, reminding him of those fireflies and old skies.

Encountering a demon was not a common occurrence, at least in the mortal realm, yet here he was, running into several of them.

But this person was not one of them.

No, a demon couldn't give someone else qi. It was impossible. The display of power Haise had just witnessed placed this individual at least within the sublime class, so they'd been trained to use the veil.

"You've saved me a lot lately," Haise ventured carefully, still flustered.

He narrowed his focus when the hand left its place and he sensed the coolness returning to his back.

"Be more careful," his saviour said, sounding a little annoyed, his tone a bit childish.

Haise had a nagging feeling that he had felt this presence before. Not solely as the voice within his mind, but as a man of darkness and whispering shadows.

There was no way to prove his hunch without seeing for himself. With a quick turn of his ankle, a back step, and a swing, his blade tipped in red, he swivelled. Faced only with emptiness he sighed.

If they were one and the same, he would have to find out another time. The mysterious veil walker had vanished, leaving Haise down an alley of blood.

Walker . . . that name suits him.

Haise felt a slight coldness as the red mist settled. Staring down the alley, he could see a wavering figure mouthing words of thanks as tears streamed down her face. Mrs Lockwood, appearing the same as she had in life, slowly dissolved into the aether.

. . .

Haise slowly made his way back to the inn. His head was an absolute mess. Unable to sort through everything that had happened, he took in the cool night air rustling through the leaves and the faint noises from town. It coaxed a wave of relaxation to wash over him.

Haise had no doubt what state he'd be in if Walker hadn't shown up in time to save him yet again. Of course, it annoyed him a little. It wasn't as though the task had been insurmountable. He should have been able to handle it alone. All these years later, he still struggled against the grip of defeat. He had promised Yasu he would become the strongest, and he hadn't.

He gazed through the windows into the inn at the people now cheering and dancing. Vallas was downing mead or some other alcoholic beverage as she battled another in a drinking game. The mood had taken a one-eighty since they arrived. What had caused it was beyond Haise.

He pushed his way through the crowds and managed to squeeze into his room. Inside, the fireplace cast warm light. Its glow fended off the encroaching night and illuminated the face of one peaceful Hiro.

Haise's disappearance must have made him worry again. It wasn't unusual for Hiro to care so much—unless your name was Lord Delfir, and then you'd get more love from a brick wall. Haise felt a teeny bit bad for him, but according to Hiro, it was strictly business between them.

"Sorry to make you worry so much." Haise spoke softly while manoeuvring a blanket over his master. A sleepy stare pinned him to the spot. *Oops . . .*

"Where were you?" Hiro immediately demanded, that caring behaviour rearing its head. Haise had done something to put himself in danger on purpose, so all bets were off, and love became something closer to exasperation.

Haise tried to redirect the conversation."Why does it feel like people are celebrating?" he asked. There was no way the demise of their local murderer had spread that quickly.

"The priestess offered a vision from the gods that a saviour would deliver divine justice by the end of the day. Now, stop trying to change the subject." Hiro knew exactly what Haise was doing, and there was no escape from his merciless interrogation.

"Playing hide-and-seek with a little girl," he said, sounding weary.

"Haise, you are terrible at hide-and-seek. What were you really doing?" Haisde had expected the jab, but it didn't lessen the blow.

"For the most part, I was, and I did my best. Apart from that, there was also a demon. A horse of death called Kuro and a strange man who could walk through the veil," he said nonchalantly, as though it were just another day.

He left out the part about a voice speaking in his head. Hiro needn't worry about his sanity. Haise was sure whoever owned it was real now, and if he were to tell Hiro, it would only burden his master more.

In any case, Walker wasn't a threat, and Haise had made sure not to insinuate he was. Given Hiro's expression, maybe his caution was unwarranted. Haise had spewed a whole bunch of crazy, and all Hiro did was sigh.

"I leave you be for a day, and everything seems to want a piece of you," Hiro said as he stretched, coming out from underneath the pelts piled on the leather chair, his decision to sleep there clearly taking its toll. "Let me look at your arm, Haise. The bandages are loose again."

Layers of white had slipped away from his arm and dangled awkwardly. Stains had leached through, sullying the white fabric. It unravelled like a talisman, tumbling off his arm as if losing hold of the curse it was binding.

"Strange," Haise mumbled. The pain had halved at some point, and the wound was healing quickly. Hiro glanced at him questioningly.

"Did you start practising medicine again?"

The query caused a sting of pain. Even if he had, it would never have been this effective. No amount of rest or time could pull him from the depths of self-doubt and guilt.

"No. I would never . . ." Haise recalled that tender hold, the brush against his pendant and the flow of heat. Unconsciously, he touched the stone, which responded with a pulsing glow.

"It was him. He killed the demon and poured qi into me." He frowned. The kindness shown by Walker made Haise want to believe they were less of a stranger. That they had become something more. *It's almost as if he knows me.*

"Tell me everything. Don't leave a single thing out," Hiro insisted as he rewrapped Haise's wound with a bandage graciously supplied by the inn.

"Of course." Haise yawned, speaking in mumbled breaths laced with exhaustion.

The amount of qi overloading his body was having an effect similar to that of an extreme sugar high. He was crashing quickly. Hiro easily picked up on this and changed direction. "You must be tired. We'll talk about it tomorrow after we leave."

It wasn't as though Haise was against discussing it, but after all the stress his body had gone through, he couldn't handle the withdrawals, and his vision went black. *Weak . . .*

# Chapter 14

After all was said and done, the priestess thanked them in the morning and bid them safe travels. Her loyal followers had collected the body of Mrs Lockwood, no doubt shocked by the mess surrounding her in that alley.

The priestess's smile was far too bright. The happiness exuding from her as she watched them leave pushed the point home. She was glad to get rid of Wulf and those consorting with demons. Haise brushed off the disingenuous display of gratitude. He found his happiness in the knowledge of their safety, not in her thanks.

Vallas had mended the cart over the period of their stay. She was a hard worker, willing to put in the effort and skilled at her craft. Haise believed she was the one who had livened the mood at the inn, causing the people to release their anxiety and finally relax. All throughout yesterday, with ale in hand and her characteristic humour at the ready, she had stayed with those coping with tragedy, and their smiles had borne witness to her success in taking their mind off their loss.

"Let's get goin'." She slapped Haise on the back, causing him to stumble forwards. He huffed a laugh as they all hopped aboard. He was concerned for the townsfolk and about the possible reappearance of Kuro. Despite that, he was grateful to be continuing their journey.

Unlike when they arrived, people wished them well and thanked their "saviour," the title unbefitting. It wasn't Haise who had saved them; it was Walker.

"It would normally take another six days to arrive in Norval, but with winter on its way, we could encounter various unforeseen issues. We'll need to rest at Falk and prepare for the harshness of the north." Hiro spoke in a questioning tone, as if he were asking Haise if that was okay.

"Right." There was nothing to be done. They would go and leave as quickly as they could.

. . .

Falk boasted a large, mansion-like inn called the Sleepy Owl. It was a far more simplistic and homely place to stay than the Bowers Inn in Hamstead, with its exotic excess.

In Helmbi, the nightlife was bright and bustling; everyone loved to be out on the streets, breathing in the delicious smells of fried food. Haise saw the same enthusiasm here, but the air was damp with the threat of incoming rain. It wouldn't be long before all would retreat to the warmth of their homes.

The majority of buildings Haise passed were newly built. However, some were hundreds of years old, still standing tall and strong. They boasted ancient features in their designs, from the peaking dormers on their roofs to their half-timbered sides, and everything still appeared to be in its prime. These homes were of a style similar to Hiro's, with wooden walls and sliding doors to let winds race through the spacious rooms. Large beams curved down the slanted roofs, laden with vines and moss.

There were eateries, a tailor, a blacksmith, a jeweller, stores selling knickknacks, and more. At the center of it all was the Clan of Falk's House of Nyal, with its famous bird messaging system. The village had no impressive commerce like Vale, but this produced an inviting atmosphere where one could slow down and be humbled by the simpler things in life.

Haise's eyes wandered until they drifted up a stepping-stone path that led away from the main road. They caught on a smaller structure surrounded by stone sculptures of little creatures. He mumbled, "Wait."

The nimako kept its pace, and as though in a trance, Haise dropped off the back of the wagon. He took each stepping stone in stride. Wulf followed his lead and tailed close behind, wondering what had consumed his partner's sole focus.

What stood at the path's end was a dilapidated shrine. The tiny whimsical creatures bowed to the deity worshipped within its once-hallowed walls.

Out of the shrine came a surprised older lady with partially scaled skin, a trait indicating she was a spirit-kissed victim. A cane followed her down the hill, supporting her limping gate. She gave off an aura, an impression of someone he used to know, as though she were a distant relative.

"Blessings be upon the Golden Healer." Her smile was warm and knowing. It caught him off guard as he reached out to the wooden frame entrance, its carved designs lost to old flames.

He turned to the space inside. It hadn't been tended to for quite some time. Haise made his way to the offering table and noticed that it was the only surface clean of dust and ash, but the air was stale.

Cobwebs had collected in every nook and cranny. The small censer was packed to the brim with long-burnt incense, and off to both sides cold candles sat in pooled wax, their blackened wicks curled over.

The offerings had included flowers, fruit, and loaves of bread, which now lay dried, shrivelled, and beyond decay. Any more-valuable offerings would have been taken back or stolen by another.

Quite some time was an understatement, Haise realised. If he hadn't bumped into the old lady in front of the temple, it would have been easy to say this deity hadn't been prayed to for at least a hundred or so years.

It wasn't often that gods fell from grace or perished in battle, but it happened occasionally. After years of having no answers to prayers, mortals would become dispirited and abandon their gods as they had abandoned them. Their shrines would fall into ruin just like this one.

He was overtaken by myriad emotions that conflicted endlessly, a battle of oil and water, desperate to mix but fated to be forever separate. One seized victory as it surfaced above all the others: guilt. He brushed the pale line on his finger, pain clamping down on his chest.

Above the table, perched on a pedestal, was an elegant sculpture of the deity. Its features were fine and delicate. The figure sat in seiza, their legs tucked out of sight. They were plucking the strings of a guqin, their lips parted as though captured in the midst of song.

Amongst the debris left by the devotees rested a couple of flowers he hadn't previously noticed. The blossoms' contrast with the neglected room was considerable, their bold colours speckled with dew, and as Haise lifted one to his nose, a gentle fragrance kissed his senses.

"An eternal flower . . . but how . . ." Hiro spoke from the entrance to the shrine. These two blossoms and a great number more grew in the mountains of Dramour. They were referred to as eternal flowers because they never ceased to bloom. What was most strange about this occurrence was that no one had gained access to the mountain's recesses since its fall. All flowers withered, and Dramour's eternal flowers were no exception to this rule. They might bloom in all seasons, but they weren't immortal. *These flowers are fresh.*

Even with this strangeness to distract him, the shrine still forced painful memories back to the surface. They came from a time when Haise had thought he could help anyone he met. No person's matter was any less important than another's. It was foolish, a childish, naive hope, but to him, that's what it meant to be a god.

Before

# Chapter 15

Just past midday in the mortal realm, the first victim of the strange disease was struck ill in Falk. A feverous child lay bedridden as local physicians argued amongst themselves, for their treatments were not working. The child's raw throat made talking a harrowing task, so silence shrouded him as his watery eyes grew swollen. His limbs weakened from fever and exhaustion, and an itchy rash caused his skin to erupt in red bubbles.

The disease spread from one to two, then from two to seven and from seven to twenty, and people started to worry if they would ever recover. The Clan of Falk called in more physicians, to no avail, and the situation degraded more.

Passing travellers did their best to avoid the village, but some brave enough saw great profit in Falk's misfortune, selling faux elixirs with an expensive price tag that ran the town dry. Still, the numbers increased, the cures had no effect, and many lost their will to fight.

Gloom fell over Falk, and the once-lively town with its renowned messaging system fell into stagnancy. Some believed all was not lost, praying to the god of health and longevity, but their hopes were answered in a different way.

A passing merchant spoke of grand tales surrounding a new god of healing, a master of medicine who could produce miracles beyond belief, as though bringing life back to the dead was child's play.

The villagers who believed did their best to rally others, but many were either loyal to the old gods or filled with suspicion. After all, being tricked repeatedly didn't leave much room for trust.

This division in beliefs began to separate people into groups. Their clan leader quelled their fighting by reminding them of their common foe. With understanding came camaraderie, albeit begrudgingly. All the people unaffected by the illness built a shrine in this new god's name: the Golden Healer.

. . .

While this was occurring in the mortal realm, each day in the heavenly realm flowed like those that came before, and Haise grew restless. Though he thoroughly understood his duties as a god, superbly upheld the dignity and demeanour his position required, and excelled in his classes with Sir Markus, his instructor, he was still manipulated masterfully by the inexcusable hold of boredom.

At first, the heavenly realm had amazed him beyond belief. The sights, the smells, the people, the buildings—nothing came close to the exquisite expansion of this realm.

As he walked the paths, people stopped to praise his skills, offering handshakes of friendship and gossiping about who was gaining the most followers. In the twist of events that were his ascension, Haise became the hot topic in everyone's conversations, and the attention was something he had never experienced before. The whole thing was exhausting, and although Haise appreciated their kind words, he wondered if any truth existed behind them.

Surrounded by so many, he'd thought he would finally feel valued. Instead, he realised it still wasn't enough. These thoughts made him feel greedy, but Haise didn't want more. It was more like the praise had no actual value and was merely pretence.

He wanted to believe this was not the case for all the people or that perhaps he had misinterpreted their intentions, but he knew they could be merciless and dubious. Still, everyone had reasons for their actions. No matter what, Haise always offered the benefit of the doubt.

He spent his days like this, conversing with his fellow deities, studying and practising under his mentor, and creating new pieces of music to play on his lyre, Akin.

Haise would sit upon the steps of his heavenly temple and pluck delicately at Akin's strings. Enchanting notes would dazzle anyone close enough to hear. His music could perform an array of different tasks, from deadly pieces that pierced the spirit to melodies that charmed and soothed.

Its shifts and changes in tone were abilities not confined to sound, as this spiritual tool could also change its physical form and morph into different stringed instruments, given it was provided enough qi.

One day, a new melody burst to life through Akinin, its guqin form. He played with the utmost care and skill, the sound nothing short of magnificent. He had completed it the previous night and was extremely pleased with how it had turned out. Its high notes were sharp but not aggressive, the low notes soft and deep. They balanced in a way that allowed their interpretation to be either happy or sad.

He had based the melody off a children's rhythm his mother used to sing many years ago but had yet to fade from his memory, and now it would be forever immortalised. As he played, he lost sight of the crowd and glimpsed the past, the shining lights and delightful smells and a boy with a joyful smile. His gut twisted, and the music halted. It was only then that he heard the pleading voices within his mind.

It was the first time since he ascended that such a significant number of people had called out to him. Surprise and joy hit him initially, but as the prayers continued, these feelings transformed into dread that washed him pale.

They weren't merely asking for good health or wishing their families well should more challenging times come. They were pleading for help, for what ailed them could not be healed by them alone.

Quickly racing through the beauty of the heavenly realm, he searched for the only god he truly trusted. Lewis Barrow was a strong individual, his greatest rival, and his best friend. They had been taught under the same lecturer and were on relatively equal footing.

He finally reached Lewis's residence. The marble-and-jade structure was the epitome of grace. Its size was humble compared to the opulent mansions of superior deities, but its ethereal beauty placed it in a category all its own.

Throughout the entire space, in beds and in pots, inside and out, grew nearly every species of plant you could imagine. The greenery flourished in the hospitable environment, its density hiding away the few heavenly creatures that considered it home.

Spiritual orbs of pulsating light amongst the foliage added a luminous glow to the surreal scene. Several small waterfalls trickled down rock formations into a pool of koi, frogs, and salamanders. The water's surface was speckled with flowering lilies and reflected light.

Each column framing the door featured a single golden peacock bending its way to the ground. The building created a sense of weightlessness, as though it were lighter than the clouds surrounding it.

The door opened before Haise had the chance to knock, and Lewis appeared in its place. Dressed casually in loose-fitting clothing, he was hard to recognise as a martial god, exceptional at archery and jujutsu. His face turned grim upon seeing Haise in a frantic state.

"Would you be willing to accompany me back to the mortal realm? They're pleading for help. I must do something, but I don't think I can do it alone," Haise implored.

Lewis sighed, placing a hand on his forehead. The cat sitting on his shoulder meowed, and a small creature with large ears peered down at Haise from within his hair.

"We were warned only recently about returning to the mortal realm, and the impacts of our influence could be drastic. Are you sure about this?" Lewis reminded him of their lecture from Sir Markus. Haise saw concern fill his dark-brown eyes, his hand slipping back to run his fingers through his black hair. The creature skittered down to his other shoulder. Wrapping a long tail around his upper arm, it clung fiercely to his shirt.

"I have to. I can't ignore their pleas. Isn't this why we ascend, so we can help those who lack the strength or knowledge to help themselves?"

"Yes, but we are not of . . ." Lewis sighed again and frowned as though conflicted. "You're right. I often think the same, but still, I dare not act too rashly." He paused again as his lips thinned and his brows furrowed.

But deliberation had been out the window from the very beginning. Haise pulled his best puppy eyes. This always worked on Lewis.

"I assume you'll require my martial arts skills?" Lewis said.

"That would put me at ease about any possible attacks while we're there. But it was actually your speech talent and your deep knowledge of flora and fauna that I thought would be most helpful. Perhaps we could find a cure together?"

Lewis raised a brow and considered this for a moment, seeming to come to the same conclusion Haise had. His talent would be valuable for gaining information from less compliant individuals. "Fine. I'll help, but you have to promise you won't do more than you must. Remember, you can't save them all. The mortal realm is tied to fate. If it is meant to be, you'll only make it worse. The last thing we want is for them to suffer more because of our presence." He adjusted the silver glasses on his nose, the chain brushing against his neck.

"I promise. I swear if I can't help, I'll swiftly return to the heavenly realm." Haise continued to plead as though Lewis's help wasn't yet set in stone.

"Mm-hmm. Got everything you need?"

Haise relaxed, affection blooming as he nodded. He touched the bladed fan at his waist as Lewis drew a teleportation sigil in the air. Its iridescence pulsed with energy as they both poured heavenly qi into the spell.

Lewis's fuzzy companions abandoned him as the shrine's entrance to the mortal realm opened. Rimmed with golden light, pools of spiritual energy cascaded down the path towards the gathering crowd.

Haise walked out of the fading glow with Lewis right behind him. The villagers' shocked mumbling was quickly replaced by grateful exclamations of "We are saved!" and "I will worship you forever," amongst other more salacious wishes whispered by several women. Their questionable intent made Lewis raise his brows.

Haise had been too eager to help these people calling out for him, and he hadn't considered the current time of day within the mortal realm. He had consequently revealed his presence, which wasn't ideal.

Lewis coughed as though understanding the predicament, prompting Haise to do something about it rather than stand there like a stunned mullet. The small crowd quieted as he stepped forwards to address them. He noticed a lack of clan colours but dismissed it for now.

"I've heard your prayers." Haise paused. He knew that picking the right words now would ease the uneasy, calm any brewing anger, and raise the hopes of those who had lost it.

"I am Alsta, a deity of healing. I cannot grant miracles or save those from the grave, but I will cure everyone here, so please worry no more. Share your pain with me, and I will lift you all from this suffering."

Some expressions were now sceptical, but most of the faces around him grew brighter with newfound hope, while Haise's grew brighter for another reason. Okay, so it wasn't his best speech, but at least they were now more optimistic as a select few guided their godly guests to the first victim of this dreadful sickness.

The buildings were well designed for the weather and shifting land. Each one had a sturdy, fieldstone foundation, and several had two stories or more. The pathways that weaved and climbed their way through town created a stone river system that spread life throughout the organised maze.

Some of these paths bravely ventured underneath buildings, the arching bridges pushing the structures up, causing homes to take on strange appearances. From them hung various plants, but passion vines took hold of the best positions and strangled any that tried to contest.

As Haise and Lewis travelled further, they passed a tall building constructed in layers upon layers as though it were a cake. It formed a unique tower with square roofs that curved to points, each roof slightly smaller than the last. Every room had a window where a single lantern hung, awaiting the night so it might illuminate the dark, erasing all animated shadows that attempted to swallow the unsuspecting.

Eventually, the group arrived at a quaint house and were greeted by a distressed mother and an anxious father. Neither of them could stop pacing.

"Lin, Michael, we have great news! These gods have come to save us!" said one of the guides who had brought Haise and Lewis there.

An older gentleman narrowed their eyes at them as Haise awkwardly raised a hand as if to wave. He promptly lowered it. "We will do our best to save your loved ones from this illness."

Lewis gave Haise an incredulous look as they stepped through the threshold past the stern old man.

The house creaked in the wake of its new guests. Its belly heaved a sigh, as though it, too, missed the warmth and happiness that had once paraded through its halls and rooms. Upon its breath wafted a peculiar smell, something sickly sweet. It was weak, as though it lingered long after the source was gone or was masked by something else. Either way, the smell was wrong and similar to another, which made Haise uneasy.

Lin was beside herself, so Michael guided them to a room towards the end of the house. Inside, a child lay covered in bedding, trying to combat the chills, and a damp cloth rested on their forehead, attempting to cool the fever. Haise went over and crouched down at the bedside. His presence hadn't drawn open the child's eyes, so Haise asked Michael, "What is your child's name?"

"Benny. His name's Benny."

Lin had been standing anxiously in the doorway, and at this, she pleaded, "Please save him. He doesn't deserve this. He's just a child."

"May I remove the covers to examine him?"

"Of course. Do whatever you must, anything at all."

"Benny, I'm just going to pull down your blankets, okay?"

No response. Haise gently pulled back the covers.

His brows furrowed at the sight of large rashes and bubbling skin, as if the fever were so hot it was boiling Benny from the inside out. The bedding was wet with sweat, and Haise felt the warmth radiating from the child as he turned his arms, checking both sides.

Many things caused a fever, but the rash was strange and unlike any Haise had seen before. This was more than a simple reaction to something the boy might have encountered, such as one of the poisonous plants that grew in this area. A child accidentally touching the wrong plant was one thing, but plenty of adults had become ill, and they would have been taught the dos and don'ts of gathering wild resources.

"How long has Benny had this fever for?" Between his shallow breathing and pale skin, Haise's two biggest concerns were the child's lungs and his fever. Benny needed water and a more aerated space.

"About eight days now, but the fever didn't come on straightaway," Lin said.

"Did he complain of a sore throat and cough often?"

"Yes. He told us, but there wasn't a lot we could give him. It pained us to see him so miserable, and as parents, to not be able to help him . . ." Michael's words caught, but Haise understood. He'd often placed himself in a position to take the pain of another, especially if it was someone he cared for.

He knew that mothers who had no access to proper medicine often used whatever was available. They would try anything and everything to save their children, but the results of their medicinal substitutions were never optimal, as was to be expected.

Haise moved on from his physical examination and placed two fingers on Benny's wrist. He immediately found his qi lacked a steady flow, and its strength was weak. It was possible Benny had been born without strong qi; however, it appeared more likely that it was being slowly drained from him, as though the boy had forgotten to tighten the tap and it dripped endlessly, spilling over into a nether world full of insatiable beasts. Haise continued to search for the tear from which the qi leaked, but this tap stayed hidden from view, so the question remained: Where was it going . . . or worse yet, to what?

If Haise were to use a healing song from *The Poetry of Purification*, it was likely to do one of two things, and neither was that great. The qi he utilised to give the song its power could simply drain with Benny's and change nothing. Or he might inadvertently feed whatever it was, making the entity stronger, possibly causing Benny's condition to deteriorate faster or bring about his demise. Using a more significant amount of qi to surpass the losses would only overload his weakened system, causing the same unfortunate result.

Unaware of the full-scale search for answers going on behind Haise's eyes, Lin and Michael watched on, anxious for a favourable outcome, but Haise knew from experience that simply wanting wasn't enough to produce success. Action was always needed, and even with that initiative, a positive result wasn't guaranteed.

He lightly touched the rose gold ring that hugged his finger. The cool surface mimicked metal, and its visible purity was of the highest quality. This was to be expected of something akin to a spiritual tool born in the heavenly realm.

"Don't. You know how it affects you," Lewis warned, but Haise knew there was no other way.

"I know," Haise whispered, a frown the only true sign of his conflict.

With his touch, the etched text began to glow, the light emanating from the heavenly words cascading across the rose gold surface, tingeing his skin and clothes with warm hues. Its plane rippled as though straining to contain the strength of the qi within.

Once the glow peaked, a great ghostly vision leapt forth, and the small light grew into a golden wash that coated the bedroom's interior. Lin and Michael gasped in awe at the sight, and Benny's eyelids lifted slightly. The creature swam through heaven's waters as though it held distant memories from when it had been within its mortal body.

The koi was pure and elegant. Its grace would never wax or wane with the moon, for time had never once constrained it. The golden visage turned to Haise and dove into his forehead. His body absorbed the light, and moments later, a third eye revealed itself.

Chapter 16

Those who saw his gaze were mesmerised. The new iris did not conform to his natural eye colour. Instead, a golden ocean poured infinitely into the pupil. His magnetism was intense, as if a sacred being hid amongst the shadowy depths peering out from within, but such was not the case. It was a simple manifestation of qi, a poor imitation at best, a mimicry of his essence. Haise agreed the creature was magnificent, but it didn't make him all-seeing. Lewis left the room as Haise began his assessment.

The third eye was temporary, allowing him to assess any damage to Benny's body and soul. Haise concentrated on detecting issues, the pupil's shape morphing from round to slitted.

The effects of this disease were devastating, and the extent of damage was now exposed. Benny's lungs were dying, almost to the point of decay, and several other organs were fighting a losing battle. Haise reined in his shock so as not to frighten the parents. Benny's predicament was far greater than he'd first thought.

He prayed Benny's soul had fared better. A damaged soul could cause substantially more agony than any flesh wound, and thankfully, it remained unsullied by the sickness. A small mercy.

"What places did Benny frequent before he became ill?" He pulled his eyes from the body, a golden stare directed to the parents.

"Well, he loved to visit Miss Maple. She's a maid at the town's inn. She often visited when she had no work, bringing over small treats and staying late." A melancholy smile crossed Lin's face. "They were like siblings."

"Did they go anywhere together?"

"Ah yes, sorry. They would go to the forest together to collect herbs for the inn, and Benny would always come home with a scratch or two. Miss Maple would always be so apologetic. We tried to tell her it wasn't her fault if Benny insisted on climbing trees, but she disagreed." Haise made a mental note to investigate these areas as well as interview any individuals who might have been venturing around the outskirts of town.

"Thank you for your help. As for Benny's condition, I'm afraid there is no fantastic news, but do not fear. I will do the best I can to help your son. For now, I suggest using this ointment for the rash."

He produced a small jar from a satchel on his waist. The paste within had been crafted by him personally and imbued with his qi to increase its effectiveness. Like Lewis, Haise also grew a plethora of plants, except all of his had some kind of healing benefit. Along with his flora, Haise had a large collection of medicinal items and utensils.

This particular creation of his contained heavenly and mortal ingredients like licorice, beeswax, and heaven's rose, among other things. Lin gratefully accepted the offer, the small jar cradled in her palm like a fragile egg of immeasurable value.

"It will ease the pain and soothe the itchiness. As for the fever, brew these herbs into a tea and have him drink it thrice daily." From the same satchel, Haise withdrew a pouch of dried herbs. Similar to the first medicine, it had been crafted by his own hand and infused with qi.

"Ensure he still eats and drinks, even if it's a small amount," Haise continued as Michael received the pouch. He bowed his head while clutching Haise's hands and thanked him repeatedly.

Haise was embarrassed by the extent of the parents' gratitude. He had not saved their child nor provided any good news. It was unlikely that Benny would recover well, but Haise would grasp this torch of hope until worsening conditions doused the flames.

The illness was perplexing. If he were to gain insight into the mystery, he would have to question the locals more. If he could find out where the infected people were or if they had consumed anything irregular, purchased anything odd from a travelling merchant, or been gifted something unusual, it could improve his chances of finding a cure.

"If I may ask, who was the older gentleman outside your house?" Haise queried. "He seemed . . . unhappy."

"That was our local physician. The only one who stayed. He's a stern man, but a good person. Don't mind him, he's just worried for all of us." A haze began to creep into the edges of his vision. Time was up.

"Thank you," Haise said as he shut his third eye, and the koi made its presence known again before returning to his ring. Dizziness threatened his composure, so he excused himself with the promise that he would find the cause of this ailment as quickly as possible.

He was caught off guard when a small gathering of people outside bombarded him. Though it made sense, it still surprised him. With the illness going around, he'd thought everyone would be inside, but of course those not privy to the knowledge of how disease could spread wouldn't necessarily be afraid of close contact with infected individuals. Plus, deities descending from the heavenly realm were a rarity. Seeing one was even less likely.

Bright eyes shone in his direction as poor Lewis attempted to ward them off. Lewis seldom showed his aura, because its depth and range were too strong. Somehow, Haise had forgotten his own status as a god.

He failed to hide his amusement at his friend's predicament. A small snort followed by a muffled laugh had Lewis giving him a deadpan look, and what immediately ensued was the halt of his security services.

Haise's brows shot up as the crowd rushed towards him. Instinctively, he leapt into the air and flipped backwards onto the roof. His training in qi flow and balance finally seemed helpful, but the dizziness made him stumble upon landing.

In his haste to examine the first victim, Haise had overused his eye and forgotten to cloak his aura. Although there wasn't much to conceal, its luminosity was blinding. He might as well have lit a fire at night or run butt naked down the street. The point is that plenty would have noticed, and so a number of them did.

He sighed and placed a hand on his head, trying to fight the waves of nausea. *Could this be any more chaotic?*

In imagining his first return to the mortal realm, Haise had thought his conduct would be at least somewhat refined and his actions more befitting a god. His hand slid away as he whispered a simple incantation to invoke the concealment and glamour spell.

"Conceal, hide from the eyes that pry."

His radiance had become so familiar he'd forgotten about it entirely. As the light spluttered and died, it left him feeling fragmented, as though he had lost a small part of himself that somehow held more meaning than he'd realised.

He abandoned his spot on the roof and headed towards the local inn. Hopefully, Lewis wouldn't be too mad that he had left him there to deal with the curious townsfolk.

Farther into the village, the only glimpses of green were potted plants on windowsills, passion vines, and the odd tree growing within the embrace of a square pot. The stone pots bore scars from chisel heads, the markings flowing into complex patterns repeated through the layers.

Here, there were far fewer people wandering the streets. This made more sense than the previous scene but constricted his ability to gather information. It wasn't as though he could barge into homes claiming to be a god and interrogate the residents for answers.

He decided he would nose around in more frequented public spaces, like the inn and local restaurants. If he and Lewis presented themselves to the House of Nyal and appeared before its patriarch, that would surely help. That is . . . if Falk still had a clan. After all, he hadn't seen any house colours, and it had been many years since his mortal days. A new type of ruling system might be in place here.

The more he roamed the streets, the stranger the situation seemed. There hung a silent truth in the air to which he was yet unaware, bringing unease to his mind. Families peering out from behind curtained windows narrowed their eyes as he walked past. The friendliness he had seen was inconsistent, leaving some more cautious and annoyed than others. Between this and the crowd earlier, the contrasts were quite stark.

He picked up his pace to avoid any possible inconveniences and arrived at the Sleepy Owl Inn. Haise had expected a building similar to those he had seen on his walk, but this abode seemed more like a country mansion. The passion vines around town had also made their way here. Tendrils climbed up all three stories and tried reaching even farther, only to be mocked by the birds and droop back down.

Stepping into the interior, he was greeted by silence. An alluring atmosphere had been created with warm and moody tones that extended to the dark oak flooring, which the traditional burning method had streaked with deep chocolate browns and blacks. But the flowing scorch lines couldn't hide all the saturated oranges in the wood.

The bar to his left proudly boasted an enormous amount of shelving for alcohol. However, the supply was incredibly sparse. The stairs to his right led to a balcony walkway where a few lanterns and clan flags hung.

His brows knitted at the flags. At least one thing was clear now: The governing system was the same, but the clan's cultivators were nowhere to be seen. Though the citizens of a town often appreciated clans, it wasn't common to see their emblems within local businesses.

Haise wondered if hanging the flags was a decision on the innkeepers' part or forced upon them by the clan. They might have merely owed the clan and not been able to offer payment or commit to acceptable terms and agreed to settle on flags to bolster the clan's image, as plenty of travellers would rest here. At least, they used to.

A clatter of noise brought Haise's attention back to the bar and the scene before him. There were enough tables and chairs to cater to the masses, but no one rested in them and the only scent of food wafted from the kitchen.

He thought back on the glares he'd received walking up here. Excluding the gathering at the shrine, he hadn't witnessed any peddlers or traders meandering about. Though there had been some homeless, none busked. *Lifeless* was the word that came to mind.

The travelling merchants had undoubtedly spread word of the town's predicament. It wouldn't be surprising if they had chosen to cease business, leaving Falk with no way to import goods and no income from sales.

Between the sick families and this likely food shortage, the silence was less shocking and more depressing. Haise was considering leaving and returning later when a cheerful young lady popped her head out the kitchen door from behind the bar.

"Ah. Hello, sorry to make you wait. I wasn't expecting any customers, so I started baking a bit." She laughed awkwardly.

"Is this establishment still accommodating guests?"

"Yes! Yes, of course. A room for one, then, sir?"

It had been years since he'd seen the symptoms of the spirit-kissed. She was human, but some aspects of her deviated from the norm. Her legs were partly scaled, like the surface of a snake caught between moultings, but instead of new bright scales, pink fleshy skin hid beneath.

It wasn't the worst case he had seen. So many cries, so many scars . . . so many he wished never to see another.

Thankfully, the prejudice had subsided over the years, but plenty of people still mocked victims for their beastly appearance.

"Could you provide a room spacious enough for two beds? A friend has travelled with me and is not currently present."

"Oh. We have plenty of rooms, as you may have noticed. Wouldn't you prefer two rooms?"

"Mm, no. One is quite all right." Haise thought it would be hard to explain that he was a god—one who had descended to raise the village from the clutches of death but had forgotten that the prices of rooms would increase over time.

He most definitely did not have enough coin. The problem was that his clothing suggested the opposite, and she was beginning to look suspicious and curious.

Haise needed to find an excuse believable enough so she wouldn't pry further. Unfortunately, his mind was utterly blank, so he blurted the first thing he thought of.

"I sleepwalk, so my friend makes sure I don't leave the room." Haise spoke so matter-of-factly that she said, "Ohhh," as though taken aback and unsure how to respond. *What was I thinking, sleepwalking? Seriously?*

There was nothing he could do now. Instead, he made an effort to change the subject. The last thing Haise needed was someone hovering around his room. After all, the concealment spell often wavered in his sleep.

"Could you include meals?" He smiled, praying she would forget this strange meeting, since his excuse seemed to imply so much worse than the truth . . .

Chapter 17

Her brow arched and her eyes shone with silent amusement as she gave him a slanted smile.

"If that's what you'd like, sir, then so it shall be. I'll be giving you room 202. Thank you for staying at Sleepy Owl and for understanding the lack of proper services. This crisis hasn't been kind to business. Most have shut up their shops. Even some families with deep roots here have been packing up to move. They seek safety in other towns, even going as far as the last stop." She spoke while approaching Haise, a deep inner conflict knitting her brows.

The "last stop" she referred to was a city by the ocean long past Helmbi to the south called Lostroth. Lewis had told him many stories of the place he used to call home. Even though thousands lived there, it was said to always be quiet.

Tales told of its whimsical people, how their lives intertwined with spirits, how they waxed and waned with the moon, and how they danced with death in sync with life and never took their eyes from the sea.

To live in such a place would be to live in another world.

"I apologise. I seem to have forgotten my manners. It is a pleasure to meet your acquaintance. I am Haise, a wandering physician who has come to assist you and your families, though I hope I am not too late."

He would prefer to keep his status hidden from those still unaware of his presence. It was far easier to investigate alone than with a group tailing him.

"Oh my, no need to worry. I'm Maple. It's a shame you're visiting at a time of great sorrow." She paused, her eyes drifting in and out of focus. "Here's your key, and dinner's in the evening. If your friend comes in, I'll bring him to the room for you."

"Thank you. I would appreciate that," he said, reaching for his pouch to procure payment for the room. When he'd finished the transaction, he followed her up the stairs.

She was about to leave him and return to the kitchen to continue baking when Haise requested she wait a moment. He had questions she could answer.

"Lin advised me that you often spend time with Benny," he began.

"Yeah. Benny. I would bake treats for him and play all manner of games with him on my days off. I'm actually baking his favourite treat right now."

"That is very kind of you." He thought back to his favourite sweet. He hadn't enjoyed a sweet bun in quite some time. "I was told that you and Benny frequented the forest. Could you tell me all the areas you've visited within the last month?"

"We only ever visit one area, the easternmost part where the ground grows uneven and the old mountain path weaves through the fog to the other side. You'll find an old well nearby and a rotten house."

"Thank you for your time. If you like, I could tell you if I find anything after searching the forest."

"It is I who should thank you." She spoke softly. "But if it's all right, I'd prefer not to know what you find. It's enough to know that you're here to help. If there's anything else you need to know, feel free to ask me or Zanita, the owner of this fine establishment. I'm certain she'd want to help as well."

"I will. Oh, and could you please bring up a pot of boiled water?"

"Of course. I'll bring up some pastries too, free of charge as long as you tell me if they taste good." She smiled kindly.

"I'm sure they'll taste lovely." He politely closed the door behind him with a quiet click. A large desk loomed at the back of the room, illuminated by the light from a square window. To the left were a sitting area, a small table with a few chairs, and a cold fireplace.

The bookshelf behind it contained plenty of genre options and random sculptured oddities. Off to his right was a room separated from the main area by two ornamental sliders.

Cutouts in the wood created an image of a bunny stretching up, still and silent, as though alert to danger.

"A motif around an owl and a rabbit . . . the bearer of wisdom and the holder of dreams." He found it curious. Now that he was alone and his thoughts less occupied, the nausea and dizziness resurfaced in uncomfortable waves.

He took a seat at the desk and dropped his head to the table, groaning. It was unfortunate that using the ring left him in such a state, but the pros outweighed the cons. He was willing to deal with the consequences, though it didn't make them any more bearable.

He was removing a sachet of herbs from another pouch on his belt when there was a knock at the door. Maple requested entry, so Haise called, "You may come in." He stood, trying to regain his composure.

"I'll leave it all on the table for you. Would you like anything else?" Her smile met her eyes, which shone with genuine care.

"Thank you, and no, I'm okay for now."

"All right then, sir. Call me if you change your mind."

Once she had left, Haise placed the sachet inside the pot Maple had left for him. The herbs turned the steaming liquid a pale amber. The fragrance was gentle and smoky with a hint of sweetness, but Haise knew this brew would be awfully bitter. They knew each other well.

Every time he drew out the power within the ring, it was too much for his body to handle, or at least that was the only explanation he could devise. No matter the cause, it was always this medicine that greeted him afterwards.

He could decide not to drink the tea, but he would be in for a night of cold sweats, muscle cramps, and nonstop voiding of his stomach. Rather than putting himself through that, he could simply add a little sugar to the tea to get it down. He never used to need it, but more recently, he hadn't been able to go without it.

He sat back down at the large desk to contemplate his next move. The warmth of tea and fresh pastries soothed his stomach, and his clouded mind cleared.

Waiting for Lewis to return before setting out to the forest would be best. It was through his friend's talent that they hoped to gain new information and a different perspective. An animal's senses could pick up on things that humans could not, and plants spoke to each other over large distances through their roots using fungal networks. If they noticed something new in the neighbourhood, it would be common knowledge amongst them all.

Daylight would soon leave the sky full of shadows, so Haise brought a finger to his lips and whispered, "Commune." Imagining Lewis in his mind, he made a connection with his friend, whose voice came booming through.

"Yeah, what is it?"

The front of Haise's head ached from the assault.

"I wanted to let you know I purchased a room for us at the Sleepy Owl Inn. I want to share what I learnt before we explore the forest."

"The forest?"

"It'll be the best place to start."

"Hey . . . you all right? You know I hate it when you use that thing."

"I know. I'll be fine. I can manage the side effects."

Lewis was silent for a moment, as if he were internally shaking his head. "I remember you telling me a while ago that you would never use it again," he finally said.

"I had no choice. I'll explain the rest when you get here." Haise rubbed his eyes, the pounding slowly easing after he severed their connection. He hated the communication sigil. Anything that invaded his headspace, invited or uninvited, gave him headaches and was genuinely disquieting. He breathed in the steam rising from the tea, the still liquid surface revealing a slightly dishevelled version of himself.

Either way, Haise was sure he could maintain his patience and composure, even in a situation that required immediate attention. He'd wait. Improving his image before leaving was necessary. He had been told as much, but things wouldn't get any worse if he did it a little later. He would wait.

To his dismay, he found himself fidgeting, his mind wandering in the uncomfortable quietness that settled over the room. His fingers seemed to move on their own. Grasping Akin, he brought to life a beautiful melody that calmed his thoughts. It appeared he could not wait. If Lewis wasn't back by the time he finished his tea or the music died, he would leave without him.

Chapter 18

Haise was looking down at the tea leaves within his still-warm cup when a knock announced the arrival of Lewis.

"Coming in, Haise."

Haise watched as the door opened to reveal his friend as well as Maple, who was laughing. The chatty pair appeared to be close. You might go as far as to think they were childhood friends if you saw them walking down the street. This was Lewis's nature: He could become friends with anyone in seconds. You could call it a talent, but Haise knew his friendliness could distract him a little and make him far less cautious.

Still, he loved that side of Lewis, a side Haise couldn't master. Other deities mocked his lack of focus. Haise believed people were ever shifting, and with there being so many viewpoints within a single person, there was never a fixity to their character.

He'd come to the understanding that observing and acting in the moment served a person better. Besides, there was always an upside and a downside to everything. Working with what you had would reveal benefits to what you'd assumed were flaws.

"Thank you for showing Lewis to my room, Maple. Also, the pastries you gave me were delicious."

"You're welcome, and I'm glad. They're a family recipe and have been made here since my great-grandma was hired to work here in these kitchens. Now, don't forget to ask for anything else you need, and if you end up downstairs in the middle of the night, I'll guide you back to bed."

Haise's smiled awkwardly as she bid them good night, and Lewis laughed his ass off.

"Looks like you won't need me after all." Lewis winked.

"I needed an excuse to cover up an unfortunate mistake."

Lewis's brows rose as he stared Haise down, his demeanour demanding a more elaborate explanation.

"I told her I sleepwalked because I didn't bring enough money for two rooms. Anyway, it doesn't matter. What matters is getting to the forest. We need to—"

"You didn't bring enough money, and you told her that!" Lewis lost himself in laughter once again as Haise turned red.

"It's not that funny!"

"Yes it is," he wheezed.

It was several minutes before Haise could tell him what he'd learnt from examining the boy and talking to the family.

The mood took a decisive turn, and they immediately headed for the forest.

Remembering Maple's directions, Haise headed east, and it wasn't long before they reached the outskirts of town. From there, they took the mountain path leading to the dilapidated house and neglected well hiding amongst the trees.

"This is the area that Maple and Benny often visited," Haise commented.

"I'll ask some of the animals and trees if they've seen anything strange lately," Lewis said before walking off in search of any willing participants. Haise searched for signs of tree climbing on his way to the structures, but there was none.

The rotting house beams had settled years ago, and the plants fought to steal the open space. The well, on the other hand, appeared disturbed. Vines sat limp around the base, as though they had lost their grip. The bucket was missing, and a frayed rope gently swayed in the breeze. The opening had been boarded up, which wasn't unusual for wells out of use. However, the wood wasn't rotting like the house and was relatively new.

He reached for the wood just as Lewis called out, "Haise, we have a problem!" Spinning, he scanned the area for Lewis, and they met halfway.

"What's wrong? Did you find something?"

"It's what I didn't find that's so concerning."

Haise tilted his head and considered this. "No animals . . . ?"

"Yeah," Lewis gravely responded.

"Were you able to find out why the animals have vacated the area?"

"Fortunately, not all the trees stood silent. A couple whispered of death in the ground. However, I'm unsure what they meant, since there are no corpses here. We would have sensed that by now."

"Could death mean something else to a tree?"

"I doubt it. It's more likely that there is some disturbance under the earth that mimics death or gives off a nasty miasma."

"The well."

"The what?"

Haise's attention returned to the well, and they drew near to the boarded-up hole.

"They look new," Lewis noted.

Haise knew the boards were suspicious, but that didn't necessarily mean he and Lewis would find what they were looking for, whatever that might be. It was possible Maple had boarded up the well herself so Benny wouldn't be too adventurous on their outings. It still wouldn't be wise to dismiss the oddity, so they began to remove the wood using *break* sigils.

Using qi, they drew small, sharp symbols in the wood, which soon glowed and pulsed with power. When they commanded "Break," the boards groaned, snapped, and shattered as though they were fragile ceramics. Most of the pieces fell down into the dark pit, and the rest tumbled off the sides.

"Ladies first." Lewis's lips quirked in amusement. Haise eyed him briefly and leapt gracefully down the tight hole, his clothing nearly grazing the mossy, damp sides. There were signs that the well had dried up, and his assumptions were confirmed as he met hard, moist ground. The missing bucket hadn't drawn water for quite some time.

The space was dark, and Haise felt small compared to its vast size, as though no walls lay beyond his reaching fingers. The soft thud behind him produced a light that blessed the newest intruders of this tiny world with sight. It kissed the rocky surfaces and illuminated the dark, baring its teeth at the shadowy beasts.

"It's bigger down here than I thought it would be," Lewis noted.

"Mm."

The area in front of them looked more like a secret ancient path one might use to escape the pursuit of an enemy force. Instead of dirt, mud, and rocks, there was a paved tunnel, and an empty metal sconce clung to the wall. From everything he was seeing, Haise doubted this space had ever been used as a well.

"It must lead somewhere." Haise let Lewis go first with the light. If "ladies first" was the rule, it would only be fair he act like a gentleman. Haise had never been quite fond of the dark, so when one tunnel opened into a cavern containing several more, he shrank at the thought of splitting up.

"What now? Should we check each one in turn?" Lewis asked as he increased the size of the light and sent it to rest on the ceiling.

"No. That would waste too much time." Haise considered his options. A search incantation would tell him if the tunnels were dead ends or if they ended up outside, though this plan was flawed. They were here to search for anything strange and suspicious, so *search* by itself wouldn't work. But it was possible to use several sigils in conjunction to produce a new outcome . . .

"Of course," Haise mumbled. He removed a slip of paper and a piece of well-used charcoal from one of his pouches. Using the wall to write, Haise began to scroll out the sigil for *create* but added a twist. He wove the lines for *spirit* within the sigil, and the two became a new symbol.

He believed his work was amateur compared to that of those who had studied the art of sigil transformation for hundreds of years. Still, he didn't need perfect. He only needed it to work.

"Lewis. Your blade, please."

The clean, sharp edge reflected the light above, and its side revealed to Haise a different version of himself, as though it were a mirror to his soul. Light pressure was more than enough to bring a small bead of blood to the surface of Haise's skin. He fingerprinted the blood onto the sigil to connect the creation to himself. Without this, nothing would stop it from killing them both, rampaging unchecked, or simply not taking orders. Almost a hundred per cent of the time, *create* required blood. Other types of incantations required a more sensual act.

There were drawbacks to many creations, but one of the most dangerous was the drain of blood. Some creations needed a sacrifice, others just a drop, and the worst in history had used hundreds of human sacrifices. This was no sigil to mess around with. However, Haise had spent several months researching and practising. He was somewhat confident in his abilities.

"Black hounds, come forth," Haise commanded. It wasn't the first time he had summoned these creatures, so he knew them and how to control them. The paper burnt. Its smoke and ash turned blacker and darker as it poured onto the floor, like hot liquid iron into a mould, forming large hounds with snarling teeth.

"Search the tunnels for anything out of place and bring it to me. Do this, and I will feed you," Haise ordered, and the hounds obeyed, each racing down its chosen path.

Echoes of howls and barks of laughter bounced back at them. The noise brought shivers to his skin. They were fast and nimble. Spirits weren't tied down by the same rules that governed the mortal realm, so when pounding feet announced their return, Haise wasn't surprised at their speed.

Of the six, only four held an object of interest. One by one, Haise collected them, and each time he gave his blood. Red droplets fell towards gaping maws, and the howling mass grew ever more excited and crazed, biting and yipping at one another before leaping into the shadows.

The smoke faded as Haise and Lewis studied the items brought forth from the tunnels. An old, shabby toy, its seams torn with stuffing hanging out. Surprisingly, a worn dagger coated in dried blood and a human skull weren't the most disturbing things here. As the two gods studied the items, one of the items studied them back.

The eye bled and rolled around within its flowery tomb. A hound had returned with a flower made of bone and flesh. Its putrid smell was like that of a rotting corpse, as if it had once been alive and now, cut away from its origins, had begun to decay.

"This plant is of demonic origins. I don't know what it is, so we should be careful," Lewis offered.

"It shouldn't be here."

"Is it possible that it was placed?" Lewis's suggestion wasn't one that could easily be ignored.

"We can't dismiss the possibility." Haise felt a surge of disgust. Had someone indeed done this? Had they understood the possible outcome, or were they simpleminded, unaware of the damage it could cause in the mortal realm? Deplorable.

"I'm not sure bringing it back with us is a good idea. Especially if this flower is what's causing all the illness," Lewis stated. The eye continued to swivel between the two as though caught halfway between madness and attentiveness.

"If it is the cause, then we'll need to study it." Haise offered an opposing suggestion with a good deal of hesitation.

"That may be true, but how do you suppose we ensure no one is further harmed in the process?" If they were to contain it somehow or nullify its effects, then Haise could discover the demonic plant's possible connection to the disease while avoiding the accidental involvement of more innocent lives.

"What about the sense-sealing incantation?"

"That would work, but Haise, I don't think that's a great idea. You'd have to stay awake the entire time." Lewis's voice was full of concern.

"Using any other sealing technique wouldn't allow us to interact with it. The only other way would be to remain in the forest. The results may not be accurate if we don't have access to stable working conditions. Taking it back is a risk I have to take."

"I know. I know." Lewis looked between Haise and the disturbing demonic plant. "Seal it. We should go back before it gets much darker."

Lewis had given in. Again.

Chapter 19

The flower was concealed within Haise's pouch in more ways than one. Even once they returned to the inn, its presence bore down on him. The smell and sight of putrefied flesh never left his mind.

As Haise and Lewis entered the inn, they were met by a new face.

"So, you're the two rentin' a room. Not what I expected."

She was tall, muscular, and much larger than Haise, so his gaze tilted up to meet hers. On the other hand, Lewis stood a chance at not straining his neck. *Rather unfair.*

Seeming to sense his childish distaste for his greater height, Lewis placed an arm on Haise's shoulder and smiled. "Why yes, we are. If you don't mind my asking, what exactly did you expect?"

She laughed and slapped him on the ass hard enough to push him forwards in shock. Haise, spared this indignity, breathed a sigh only to quickly choke on it as she said, "Well, a married couple, of course! Ya did only rent one room! Not sure where you're from, but that ain't normal round here."

"Um . . . Zanita, remember . . ." Maple tried to bring her boss back on track.

"Right you are! There's somethin' I oughta tell ya." She took a few paces back and kicked out her feet, landing hard on one of the wooden chairs surrounding a table newly decorated with flowers. Haise was surprised the poor chair could withstand the impact of such a force and impressed that the shock wave somehow left the flowers vertical with only a subtle wobble.

"Some folk say they've seen a woman walkin' round at night. It's got the whole lot on edge." Zanita spoke with no interest as she crossed her butch arms. Haise was confused. Why would a woman walking around at night cause people concern?

Before he could ask this question, she added, "With only half a face and shredded clothes." When Haise toured the village, he'd noticed the townsfolk stayed indoors. Was it not to escape the sickness but to hide from something they believed more sinister?

It wasn't common for people to see ghosts, and almost all mortal tales of encounters were horrific, although, just as with anything else in this world, there were always exceptions. Haise knew he would have to find out what this ghost was doing here and if their presence was somehow linked to the disease. It was then that he considered the flower. It was possible—no, it was almost inevitable—that this ghost knew something about the demonic plant.

"She appears only at night?" Haise queried.

"Yeah."

"Has anyone approached her or been attacked by her yet?"

"Nah. It's like she's in her own little world."

"Does she always walk the same paths?" Lewis showed his own interest.

"I don't know. I ain't got time to watch some dead girl wander the streets."

Haise decided it would be best to leave the questioning about the ghost at that, since it was unlikely Zanita knew anything more than what she'd already said.

"Okay. Thank you for letting us know. We'll try and relieve you of your ghost problem as well. Before we take our leave, Maple, could you tell me if you've recently boarded up the well in the forest?"

"The well? No, it looked like it had been boarded for years before I started going there. Why?"

"The boards appear new. Perhaps someone else has taken the time to ensure it's safe? Do you know anyone who might do something like that?"

She seemed to consider this momentarily before saying, "Samuel. He's the local craftsman. I often see him chopping wood in that forest. His house borders the forest edge to the northeast. If anyone were to go out of their way to do that, it would be him."

Haise smiled and thanked her. He headed towards the stairs, grabbing Lewis by the arm as he went.

"There are fresh pastries and boiled water in the room, but if you need anything else, let me know," Maple quickly added. Lewis smiled as he nodded his thanks, and Maple blushed.

"Weird bunch, them," Haise heard Zanita say as they climbed the stairs.

He flung the door open to a room smelling of spiced pastries and awash with incandescent light from the fireplace. Once inside, with the door closing on its own, he spun around and said, "The flower. What if there's a connection between the ghost and the disease!"

"I thought the same. Though I didn't feel the need to drag you out of the room to explain that." Lewis's brow rose. Haise smiled sheepishly. He had gotten excited about a possible lead in a situation that was becoming increasingly weird.

"To know for sure, we'll need to capture and interrogate the ghost," Lewis added.

"Going after this ghost will help me stay awake. I won't have a chance to fall asleep running through the town streets."

Lewis glanced down to the pouch containing the flower, the sealing incantation keeping its malice under lock and key.

Ridding the town of this ghost might be enough to calm the people. At the very least, it might bring them out of hiding.

With a couple of pastries in hand, they leapt with ease down from their window to the road below. It wasn't clear how fast this illness was spreading. Time was of the essence. To Haise's dismay, it was necessary to split up and search separate areas.

Somehow, the night brought an even quieter town, so cold and barren it felt void of life apart from the lanterns, which burnt warm and blazed with the energy of a hearth. Through the streets, he searched until finally he spotted a woman in an ethereal dress flowing in a nonexistent wind. The garment had gradually yellowed with age, from the bodice to its generous sweep. Her tattered shirt made the vision of her approach all the more troubling.

She continued her slow walk down the path towards Haise as though she had not seen him or had no care for his existence. Leaping back, he drew his fan, prepared for the worst while hoping for the best. Every blade was pristine, and its surface shone with reflected lantern light, its many edges honed to perfection.

She continued her approach, and Haise sensed something was off. Instead of attacking, he relaxed and stepped aside as she walked past. There was no sign of aggression, but there was another more terrifying revelation to add to this growing web of mystery.

White stitches stood stark against her mottled grey skin. Her lips were bound by a curse.

 Chapter 20

Within the heavenly realm, a magnificent library stood proud and overflowed with knowledge in the form of books, scriptures, letters, tomes, pictures, and even some ancient artefacts floating gently above marble pedestals. When he wasn't playing his lyre, Haise often preferred to rest there and indulge in the secrets of the world. He had read of this curse in a tome kept in the library but had never considered its use on a ghost.

Most known cases of this curse being used involved the subjugation of mortals, usually by other mortals. This particular curse should work only on the living, making what he'd just seen an impossibility. When Haise thought about how someone could pull this off, he came to one conclusion: Somehow, somewhere, a part of this victim lived.

Most curses had a kind of flaw, whether it lie with the victim, the curse itself, or the caster.

The flaw here wasn't with the caster or the curse. For one, Haise knew this curse didn't require blood or anything else from the caster as a means to bind the curse. So there was no way to track the caster.

As for the curse, it was well done. At a glance, nothing appeared wrong or weak enough to tamper with. It was always possible to find something of the sort on closer inspection, but that was hard when the victim might or might not want to murder you. In this particular curse, the flaw lay with its victim. A greater strength of will or desire could break the curse's hold. The caster had circumvented this flaw by removing the victim's humanity. No matter how aggressive or sullen she was, there was no escape if there was no will.

The caster knew what they were doing and had the skill to pull it off.

With dread, Haise connected to Lewis once more. "We might have a problem. I found the ghost, but I doubt we'll learn much from it."

"Why is that?"

"Does 'The Internal Prison' sound familiar to you?"

"The ghost has been cursed . . . but how? For what purpose?"

"Weird, right? We might need to monitor her, especially if any developments connect her and the illness."

To break the curse, they could find and kill the remaining part of the victim that lived, but such a task could take years, and these people didn't even have weeks. Haise wondered if there was any other way.

Since she wasn't a complete ghost, perhaps a tiny portion of will clung to the idea of retribution. If it were brought to the surface with some coaxing, they might stand a chance of temporarily alleviating her blight.

Following the ghost from behind, he assessed its state. The victim possessed the appearance of someone aged by centuries. To be in such a state upon death wasn't likely, but not impossible either; in such a case, the ghost would be considered to be lingering. This would imply higher instability or malicious intent, yet Haise could see no extreme aggravation, no indiscriminate or focused aggression.

She should be showing at least some discontent if she had been roaming for years without entering the demonic realm. Instead, she seemed almost confused or lost, which could have something to do with the curse. There were a couple of marks that stood out on her body. One indicated the cause of death; the other was the red stain dripping from her stitched mouth.

A ghost that hadn't crossed realms or moved on would typically hold on to some aspect of its life just before it died, as though still grappling with the lapse in reality. Hiding what had caused them to perish was common, especially if they were unaware of it. Based on the fact that she wasn't, this individual knew she was dead.

A stab wound to the head suggested murder. In her hand, she tightly grasped an item. It was too hard to make out, but it appeared soft and torn, as though it were a piece of something, not a whole.

The mouth wound bled continuously, as if she were trying to speak, tearing her mouth open time and time again, leaving no rest for it to heal. Something more sinister was at work here, and the notion made Haise uneasy. He feared her connection to the sickness might be far more than he'd expected.

Lewis leapt down from a rooftop and joined Haise in following the ghost. She was unfazed by the extra company, neither seeming to care nor to notice. After a while, it was evident that the ghost had no clear path or destination.

They would learn nothing new from continuing their shuffling pursuit. Haise reached forwards to tap the ghost on the shoulder to see if that would gain her attention. Before he could make contact, he was suddenly interrupted.

A burst of spiritual energy erupted before them, and the ghost dissipated, leaving a gleaming sword in its stead. Said sword then turned towards them, and its wielder declared them miscreants on account of the many misconducts they had apparently committed.

The swordsman wore the official clothes of Clan Falk and proclaimed himself the son of the patriarch Malachy Perch, after which he lowered his sword, declaring that Haise and Lewis should be thankful for his timely rescue.

He was the first clan member Haise had seen, and he already wished he hadn't. To alleviate the situation, Haise thanked him, even if his assistance wasn't the slightest bit helpful. Lewis barely held back a sneer before they both turned to leave.

"Where do you think you're going?" The official pulled them both back by the shoulder.

"To the room we've rented in the inn," Haise explained.

"Absolutely not. You're both coming with me to the House of Nyal. You have some explaining to do, and I'm sure my fa . . . I mean, Lord Perch will want to know why you're about at night in town consorting with a ghost and doing god knows what else."

Lewis snorted at the unintended truth behind his words, and Haise began to follow him. The swordsman continued to talk about how great his clan was and how grateful they should be that he had been there to save them.

It turned out his name wasn't "Son of Malachy." It was Bracken, and according to Lewis, Bracken was a dickhead. He remarked to Haise over their communication link that they should leave. Haise side-eyed him and puffed out a sigh, acknowledging the headache this situation had caused.

Leaving this man would be simple, and greeting the lord of the House of Nyal during waking hours whilst unrestrained by misperception would be in their best interest, especially if they wished to gain the clan's favour and support in the future.

Then again, if they left now and came back later, they could be under more suspicion when Bracken recognised them and points out their misdeeds to all those present. Haise whispered back to Lewis in his mind that Bracken might be unreasonable, but at least they were headed to the House of Nyal. It was now or never.

Weaving through the town, Bracken brought them to the estate of Clan Falk. There was very little stone used in the walls and buildings, and when Haise spotted some, he saw it had been shaped beyond its nature. Most of the buildings matched the town's dislike for spreading architecture, standing three or more stories high. In various places, great passion vines climbed to the heavens and bore light-purple flowers.

They would be taken to the House of Nyal, which was presumably located in the middle of the estate if it followed the pattern of other clan houses Haise had seen. He wondered what floor or room they would head to if that held true here.

When they arrived, the house was enormous and boasted three multistory towers, each level boasting its own curled roof with hanging ornamentation.

Two stone-faced guards pulled the double doors wide, revealing a surprisingly expansive space lit by elegant wall sconces, their fire flickering in the sudden draft. They were met by a meek young lady who presented herself as Lord Malachy Perch's private maid. Bracken's treatment of her was demeaning, yet she politely escorted them to the household's greeting hall. Haise wondered if he had a reason to be so rude. Jealousy, perhaps? Either way, he believed such a tone shouldn't be taken.

She entered the hall before them and stood well behind the seat upon which the lord sat. At first, he appeared tired, but there was anger and strength behind those scanning eyes.

His hand rose just as Bracken was about to speak. Bracken's mouth snapped shut, and with a flick of the lord's hand, his knee fell to the ground as he dropped to an unexpected bow. Haise was startled by the boy's obedience, so opposed to his previous displays of vanity.

"So, I hear you consort with ghosts. Care to explain yourselves?" The lord's tone was flat, and he took no liberty to mask his discontent.

"First of all, we don't *consort* with ghosts," Lewis said, enunciating the part about consorting as though he were offended by the accusation. Haise, on the other hand, wasn't fazed. He believed they kind of were.

"We are here to free your town from its sickness, and it just so happens that there is a possibility your ghosty is somehow involved," Lewis continued. Haise glanced at him.

If Lewis's annoyance were any more visible, white curls of steam would be puffing from his nose.

"Many people have passed through claiming they were here to help." Lord Perch sounded half defeated, half angered. He rose from his chair and stepped towards them. "All have failed or lied. What makes you any different from the rest?"

Lewis narrowed his eyes, unaware that Haise had begun muttering the reversal incantation without hesitation or consideration: "Reveal; show what must be seen."

The room was engulfed by light so powerful the flames bowed their heads. It swallowed everything, like a storm wreaking havoc upon them, as lightning fractured through the air.

The darkness flowed back in mere seconds, creeping into every nook and cranny. It returned all but one shadow to their rightful places. Haise stood apart from the darkness, his skin emanating a thin layer of that shocking light.

This glow elevated his appearance significantly, but Haise wondered if this show of meagre power would be enough to sway the lord's opinion. He hadn't moved from where he stood, but Bracken had fallen back on his ass and was now inching away from Haise. The lord narrowed his eyes in scrutiny.

"I cannot stand before you and say we will save them all, but as a god, I will do my best by your people," Haise asserted.

At this, Lord Perch huffed. "Fine. If you believe you can make a difference, by all means try. Today has been too long. I must retire again. See yourselves out."

And with that, they were dismissed.

 Chapter 21

"That could have gone better," Haise admitted as he cloaked his aura again.

"Ya think? What was that back there? Were you trying to blind the guy? Sure, showing your presence as a god wasn't a bad idea, but to decloak right in front of them? If your control had slipped even for an instant, they'd both be ash!"

"So, all's well that ends well, right?"

"Seriously?"

"Okay, okay. I'm sorry, but would he have let us go if I hadn't done that?"

Lewis paused and considered this a moment before sighing. "No . . . but I'll still make you pay for the shock you put me through." As Lewis spoke, an ominous yet playful smile grew on his face.

Haise laughed nervously. Lewis lunged to grab him, and Haise dodged. The two parried the whole way back to the inn, grinning as they swiftly moved through the silent streets.

. . .

Diving straight into a discussion of what they planned to do going forwards, they came to an understanding that much had to be done in a very short amount of time. Breaking the curse on the ghost was out of the question, but if she were to appear again, there was a chance Haise could dampen it for a brief moment.

When the ghost was partially freed from her chains, Lewis could carefully pry information meaningful to their investigation out of her. Haise knew this sounded awful and cruel, but it would have to be done if they had the chance. An underhanded trick like this could save many lives, but it would never save hers.

Unfortunately, the likelihood of seeing the ghost again after Bracken's introduction was abysmal. In the meantime, they would focus on going door to door at sunrise, providing the citizens with symptomatic relief. Once this was done, Lewis would aim to retrieve information from the ever-friendly lord about all the deaths and missing persons in Falk's history.

Haise would find Samuel and ask him if he had done anything around the well recently. He also needed to study the demonic plant. There were many tests he could do, but with limited equipment and time, he hoped discovering the secrets it held would be easy. His head felt heavy as the tasks continued to pile on.

In their room, Haise pulled out the grotesque flower in his pouch and was again disgusted by its appearance. The sealing spell worked even if the flower parts were separated. The sense-sealing incantation worked on a few human senses, including smell, sound, and touch. For some reason, it couldn't hide things from taste or sight.

He was eternally grateful for the lack of smell as he carefully relieved the flower of its petals and separated them into different dishes. The eye stayed fixed on him. It was an incredibly uncomfortable experience.

Even as he removed the eye from its fleshy socket, it stayed open, seemingly aware of its predicament. Before Haise could ask Lewis for help, his friend had already gone down and retrieved a bottle of liquor. Haise saw it had an absurd concentration of ethanol as Lewis passed him a glass.

One might have believed it was an invitation to drink, but Haise was an extreme lightweight, and Lewis knew him well enough. A single plop sounded as he dropped the eye into the solution. It bobbed like a rotten egg, an object well beyond its use-by date. Just in case, he filled another container with candle wax to seal it in after taking samples.

Who knows, maybe I'll need it later? Haise shivered at the thought.

Lewis looked over Haise's shoulder at the stem laid out before them. Expecting normalcy at this point would be ridiculous, but Haise was ever the optimist. His positive thinking didn't change the nature of the stem. Where most plants had a fibrous green stalk, this one was made of bone.

One vertebra after another, it stretched like a spine. The niche they had tried to confine this organism within was too small for its attributes. The demonic flower fit within the worlds of both flora and fauna.

Skin as petals, vertebrae as stems, ribs as leaves, blood as fluid. The eye was a more curious feature, and Haise didn't see the relation. He felt Lewis bend further over as he reached for the glass containing the eye.

"I may not know this particular demonic flower, but if I had to guess, I'd say there's pollen inside this." Lewis spoke as he moved the glass to the centre of the table.

Haise was shocked by his timing. It was almost a little creepy. He would have known if he had left the communication line between himself and Lewis open, as he would be feeling rather unwell. Haise narrowed his eyes.

"What?" Lewis said.

Haise was quiet for a moment. "You were reading me, weren't you?"

When Lewis used his communication talent, it was less verbal and more along the lines of thought-provoking. Using heavenly qi, his mind entered the qi flow of another. Once in, he made suggestions to the being. In turn, these caused the individual to "think" or "feel" certain things. Lewis picked up on these signals and read them like an open book. He held the master key to every mind in the world, but not everyone was so naive, and some could feel his presence.

This wasn't a problem for him, since he could talk verbally and psychologically at the same time. His skill was so effective that all but the strongest of minds become putty in his hands. Lewis's ability to handle such a complicated task made the other deities detest him more.

To Haise, he was an irreplaceable friend, and this perk just happened to be a part of him. After all, it was Lewis who could gain information from a tree. Without him, life would be a little bit harder and a whole lot darker.

"And? You were keeping your thoughts all to yourself and just staring at it," Lewis argued.

"Lewis . . ."

"Yeah. Yeah, I know. Under no circumstances, unless for emergencies, should one ever invade another's private thoughts or cause them to think differently," he said while holding one hand up in a pledge, mocking the notion with a sarcastic tone.

"Have you tried speaking to the flower?"

"I have. It thinks of nothing but devouring. I receive no normal response. It's like speaking to a living corpse, incoherent and foreign."

Haise mulled it over. Yet another barrier had arisen to what could have been helpful insight.

"So, you think there might be pollen in there."

"I'd bet you on it, and if I win, you have to . . ." He paused and thought about his prize. "Write me a song! You're always writing pieces of music, so I want one dedicated to me, okay? Promise."

Haise chuckled. Lewis was far too carefree. If the nature of the eye was anything like Lewis thought, their problem was about to magnify in severity. Haise feigned a smile.

"Promise. Now go fetch more tea," he said, shaking his head and pushing Lewis off his shoulder. Haise sliced the eye open as his friend sauntered off, and tiny yellow beads flowed out. They pooled like blood and stained his mind with worry.

Haise knew there was much for Lewis to be annoyed over. He had dragged him out on this selfish endeavour. He had made him go against the heavens. If fulfilling his promise would make him happy, Haise hoped it would be enough to compensate for his help.

"I guess I'll be writing you some music when we return," he said as footsteps sounded behind him.

"While I enjoy music, I don't believe you intended that for me." Maple spoke softly as she placed the tea on the low-set table near the fireplace. Haise stood quickly, brushing the eye and its contents into his hand. Turning to face Maple, he kept his hands behind his back and sidestepped to block the rest of the specimen from view.

"Do forgive my rudeness. I wasn't expecting you. Thank you for the tea, Maple. May I ask where Lewis is?" he said, wondering to himself, *What was he thinking, sending Maple up here?*

"He thought you might be concerned, since he is to be watching you"—*Thank you, Lewis,* Haise thought sarcastically—"and he told me he wouldn't be long. There was just something he needed to check."

"Is that so? Well, at least he told you where he was going." Haise wondered just what he could be up to.

"No, unfortunately, he didn't say. I apologise for disturbing you. Please enjoy your tea." Maple slipped away.

Haise was confused as to why he had spoken to Maple and not him directly. They had a plan that allowed both of them to know what the other was doing, and where, and when. If an emergency ever happened or something unusual occurred, they would open the communication line.

It must not be important.

Still, it wasn't like Lewis to leave people in the dark. He loved to talk and share. Whatever it was, it was new, so new that Lewis hadn't had time to communicate, or something had caught his eye and whatever it was was on the move.

Haise turned, goop slipped unpleasantly through his fingers, and he almost gagged as the eye pooled on the table.

He looked from his hands to the window. Buildings loomed over his view of the forest, but the sky peeked above it all with twinkling lights. Lewis would be fine, and Haise was sure he could handle his own sleepwalking just for tonight. With his blade in his wiped hands and a well-brewed pot for company, his studies continued until the break of dawn.

 Chapter 22

Haise yawned as the birds swooped through the forest bower and sang a melody to the changing hues on the horizon. To keep the sense-sealing spell in effect, Haise hadn't slept a wink. Much to his annoyance, Lewis had stolen to bed sometime in the middle of the night.

Haise tidied up the table and cast a spell of illusion on the pieces of tissue and plant. He didn't want Maple to stumble on them if she decided to dust or bring them more pastries and tea. The incantation allowed the caster to change the appearance of what they could see into whatever they desired.

As expected, there were a few drawbacks to the spell. You needed a complete view of the changing subject and to have previously seen every angle of what you wished to create an illusion of. The illusion spell hid from sight but would never conceal from any other sense, which was its most bothersome flaw to deal with. There were others, but they were more obvious; for example, an illusion of air could not be achieved, and an illusion could not be cast on another illusion.

Haise's samples, implements, and texts were transformed into books, pens, an inkwell, and a vase of flowers. These were items he believed to be of no interest to anyone. The last thing he needed was for someone to move them or accidentally steal them.

"Morning. How did the examination go?" Lewis asked as he opened the shoji that separated the bedroom from the main room.

Another yawn escaped Haise. "Most of the flower seems to lack purpose as a floral organism. As you know, flowers are designed in a particular way to attract certain species. I'm having trouble understanding how it would achieve this. The flesh appears like petals, but the shape and colour are of no relevance. If we consider the entirety of the flower as a food source, is there anything that would eat it?"

"Well, any scavenger would likely go after it because of the smell, even if the shape is odd. Things like foxes, birds, rats, flies, large—"

"What about the Nyal?" Haise interrupted, his stomach dropping as he spoke the name of the messenger birds. "If it did, someone could have done this purposefully, knowing what would happen."

"I suppose the Nyal is an omnivore, but it's more likely to go after Passiflora flowers and fruit than . . ." Lewis stared at the illusions as though he could still see the grotesquery hidden beneath.

"The flower, if it were coloured in a similar way, would look almost exactly like a stemmed larger Passiflora flower. The Nyal would no doubt eat the demonic plant if it were to see it."

Haise was beginning to see the impressive nature of this entity. It existed as fauna with transformative traits more in line with flora. Given that it was a possible predator, its design and function became all the more worrisome. In all aspects, it was as though it had no flaws and, with that, no cure.

The whole country faced impending doom if the birds were to eat it and continue their work. Haise and Lewis needed to alert Lord Perch immediately and halt the entire messaging network. The birds must not leave their aviary until it was confirmed that the flower was either not a threat or had been completely neutralised.

"Lewis." Haise's tone held great urgency, so much that Lewis leapt into action, disappearing in a flash. If anyone could sway someone with words alone, it would be Lewis, but knowing him, there'd be a sprinkle of nonverbal persuasion.

Haise gave one last glance at the table before leaving himself. He was at once both hoping Samuel knew about the flower and dreading finding out that he did. He had a sinking feeling when he considered the possibility of Samuel's involvement, but Haise never jumped to conclusions.

He felt he was missing something. If Samuel had known Maple and Benny played in the area, he might have blocked off the well for their safety. If he didn't know, why border off an old well far from your home?

Either way, Samuel had likely covered the well. He would have already come into contact with the growing darkness beneath. Yet again, time was of the essence.

. . .

Samuel's house was more secluded than Haise had thought it would be. A short path led to a home nestled amongst trees. It was a quaint cabin, nothing like the impressive buildings in town. With rustic stonework and moss-covered logs, it held a different charm, and like a vestigial limb, it was old but not forgotten as it humbled itself around the might of nature.

Haise knocked on the wooden door, and it slowly opened. *Well, that's not ominous . . .*

He stepped over the threshold, hoping Samuel would forgive him for the intrusion. Fresh-cut flowers sat in a vase on the kitchen table, the walls were lit with weak lantern light, and a silent chill had settled deep into the heart of the home.

"Samuel! Samuel, are you here!" Haise heard no response. The man might have left early to retrieve wood for his craft, but a cold pot of soup on the fireplace trivet made Haise wary. Something was off.

He turned his attention to the shaded woods and the trail that snaked into its shadows. Haise hesitated as demonic qi tendrils seeped from the soil and warped the air around his feet. New thoughts arose, stemming from his concern about the source of this qi, and they began a merciless attack against any hope Haise had feebly clung to.

Desperate to shake off the waves of doubt and unease, he weaved along the path until his feet met with those of the craftsman. It was as he feared. His hope died as he confronted the harsh truth.

A fallen tree blocked the way forwards . . . and the view of Samuel's other half. Haise had to take a moment before crouching and examining what he could. Gently, he touched Samuel's hand and searched for life with his own qi. He received no response.

"I'm sorry. I was too late. Forgive me." He bowed his head. If he opened his third eye, he would know the extent of the damage to Samuel's body as well as what had killed him in the end. Using it once was taxing on his mind and body. To use it again might not be so wise, given his predicament.

Frustration bore down on Haise. Qi lines could only tell him so much, and it wasn't going to be enough. The conundrum was annoying, but he at least had enough knowledge to settle for a more intrusive approach.

"I apologise in advance for this." Desecrating the dead wasn't something Haise had thought he would be doing today, but if the insides of Samuel could provide some clue as to the origins of the infection, then an apology was all he could offer.

Before he began the impromptu autopsy, he carefully removed the few flowers sprouting from Samuel's body and kept a couple more eyes, making sure to seal them. Haise believed one could never be too careful, and after delving into the literal bloody mess, he discovered a new strangeness to add to the ever-growing list.

Within every blood vessel, a vine-like cord could be found. It reminded him of the string one might find in a puppet dancing on the whim of its master.

The skin had sunken in places with black putrefaction, which at first brought to mind the normal decomposition seen after ten or more days, but Samuel's body was still bleeding. Haise scrutinised the two sections the body had been divided into. *What could possibly cause such a vast difference in . . .*

Nausea consumed him as he watched thousands of tiny vine tendrils devour flesh. The blackened areas were seething in vines, and from these areas bloomed the grotesque flower. He had seen several dangerous demonic plants and creatures before, thanks to Lewis. However, only a few could compare to the depth of this one's depravity.

Similar to parasites, it had gradually taken control of Samuel's movements and begun eating him alive. Haise was reminded of Benny, and the quick degradation of his condition now made sense. It all proved the limits of his third eye. What had happened to Samuel was Benny's reality, a cold and unyielding truth. Death was close, and Haise had to move faster.

Looking down at the corpse, Haise knew he had to stop any possible spread. Even if Samuel was quite a distance from town, there was a chance someone might eventually come looking for him. Plus, Haise really didn't want to push the whole desecration thing further by leaving the poor guy flapping in the breeze. There was the possibility of him turning into a malicious ghost, hell-bent on revenge, if Haise were to treat him the wrong way.

He extended a hand and whispered, "Incendium." *Here's to hoping Samuel is a reasonable man.* Just in case, he grabbed a few innocent flowers that grew close by. Sure, they were weeds, but to Haise, they spoke of a wild beauty that those tamed couldn't muster. Just as he placed the last few before Samuel's body, a bloodcurdling scream pierced the air.

Chapter 23

He took off running, swiftly navigating through the streets and over buildings. It was then that he glimpsed Lord Perch and a strange tall figure in an alleyway. Haise was going too fast to pause, and the scream had not come from them, but the sight was eerie enough to raise suspicion. The most disturbing part was the gaze that fell directly upon him. The tall man gave a wicked and devious smile as he bowed to Haise.

Shaken by the interaction but determined to stay on course, he located the source of the dread-inducing sound. A woman cried as she backed feverishly away from a hunched-over man. Fingers bore into skin and red dribbled down his neck as his hands tightened further. The man was choking himself.

Haise moved quickly, scooping the woman into his arms and out of harm's way. She simultaneously protested and wavered on the edge of shock, as though she were coming in and out of consciousness, her sanity slowly slipping from her grasp.

In a bid to understand or perhaps believe another truth, she mumbled, "My husband, no. No, not him. He was . . . we were just . . ." She trailed off with a blank expression as Haise leaned her back against a wall several houses down.

Leaving her here in this state felt cruel, but he didn't have time. The man was now on his knees as Haise approached, as if caught between praying for untold sins, trying desperately to appease the gods, and reeling from the knowledge that none could save him from this existential threat.

The man had tried to take matters into his own hands, but the flower had other ideas and took control. The puppeteer had brought silence down upon his world. Haise was too late again.

The corpse twitched and slumped as jerking movements brought about a disturbing scene of reanimation. Skin pulled tight as flowers broke through its surface, eyes peeking behind unfurling petals. Haise's own eyes widened as he dodged the charging man. He was surprisingly fast for a dead guy.

The light sound of bones clattering together sent a wave of calm washing over Haise, a brief cold and hollow moment of ethereal awareness. He'd felt this before, a weightless sense that stole his mind and woke the dormant beast inside him to focus on an innate primal reaction. Haise whispered an incantation; fire bloomed in the man's chest as predator became prey, the parasites falling to the mercy of an all-consuming flame. His movements were swift and elegant, like those of a dancer.

Those who saw this from inside the safety of their homes were shocked by the sudden brutality. Haise saw it in their weary gazes, but instead of rushing to explain, he knelt down near the burning man and gave him the answer to the prayer he seemed so desperate to finish.

The woman had come stumbling over and slumped next to Haise, crying out in pain, a feeling Haise knew too well. Eventually, people trickled out of their homes and joined them, half curious and half stunned. Everything but the man's bones had almost turned to ash, so there was no risk to the others.

"I implore you all to understand this disease is like nothing I've ever seen before. I promise you, I am close to a cure." Haise knew he had to tread lightly here. A white lie might be useful to quell their fear, but telling too many would weave a dangerous web.

"If anyone is experiencing symptoms of fever, nausea, rash or burning skin, coughing, or anything new or unusual to your health, please . . ." Haise looked at each person as they spoke amongst themselves. "Please tell me. I can provide immediate relief to these symptoms now while I continue creating the cure." Haise worried none would come forwards, but one after another, they began voicing their concerns, either for themselves or for a family member.

As promised, Haise treated their ailments. Faces were relieved of pain and worry; patients and their loved ones breathed sighs of relief. Haise had made sure to pack as much medicine as he could from what he'd been able to make overnight.

"I want to help as many of you as possible, but I am only one person. So I'll be setting up a treatment zone in the middle of town near the Sleepy Owl Inn. Please go there if any new symptoms occur and your condition worsens. Severe cases will be brought into the inn and placed in isolation.

"If possible, tell your neighbours, friends, or anyone who doesn't already know. We need to help each other now more than ever." Haise spoke earnestly. He needed them to understand, be careful, be aware, and encourage others. In all this tragedy, he hoped this could keep them strong.

He had to return to the inn. It was likely Lewis had come back from his trip to Lord Perch's estate, but Haise wondered if he had been able to meet him. He should find time to tell Lewis about the strange person he had seen talking to the lord, but first, there was something he had to make sure of.

"Could someone look after this young lady until she feels well enough to return home?" he asked. The woman was still slumped over near her husband, fat tears rolling down her rosy cheeks. She needed consoling, a shoulder to cry on, and perhaps a nice hot tea. He reached down and scooped her up again.

"We will."

Haise turned to see Michael, Benny's father. He must have heard the commotion and come running down the street to see if there was anything he could do.

"Michael. How are Lin and Benny faring?" Haise asked gently as he placed the woman in Michael's arms. She had fainted or fallen asleep from exhaustion. They were both likely infected, so he was glad Michael had been the one to volunteer rather than someone who was perfectly healthy, even if such a thought was not kind.

"Lin is . . ." His face was grim. "She has a fever, but she won't rest. She's beside herself. Nothing I say or do seems to console her. Benny isn't rolling around in pain anymore, and his fever is gone. Even so, I fear his stillness more." Haise knew what would happen to Benny, but he couldn't bring himself to tell Michael. The truth was too shocking, too painful.

"If you can, keep her outside on a bench. Here, take this for the woman, Lin, and extra for Benny, in case his symptoms return." Haise placed the last parcel of medicine he had prepared in her lap. "It's no cure, I know. I'll do my best for your family and everyone else in this town."

"I know you will."

. . .

Lewis was waiting outside the inn when Haise returned. Haise thought it odd that he hadn't shown up when the woman screamed or tried to use the communication sigil to ask what had happened. Lewis was a very nosy person and loved knowing what was happening to everyone at every point.

"So, how did it go? Did you manage to get Lord Perch to halt the messaging system?" Haise asked, a brow rising as though he were questioning more than just that.

"Absolutely. Let's just say, when you can't think of anything smart to say, say something funny."

"What did you do . . ." Haise was perturbed by his tone but intrigued by the circumstance until he realised Lewis probably had done something underhanded. "You know what? Never mind, I never asked."

Lewis made the gesture of zipping his lips and winked. Haise sighed.

"On another note, I saw a strange man in the alley just a moment ago, and he was with the lord. That's why I wondered if you had been able to see him in the first place."

"Huh. I also saw someone strange lurking around last night, so I went to investigate but found nothing I thought worth mentioning. All I could sense was a trivial amount of residual demonic qi, as if someone had cast an incantation."

"If it's the same person, we should keep our guard up. They didn't seem savoury, and it appears they have connections to Lord Perch. We should consider being more careful around him as well. Perhaps you could find a way to learn more about their relationship. Though I hate to think it, it may be possible that Lord Perch has something to do with this."

"Dealing with unsavoury characters would lead anyone to think that. I'll see what I can do, but between what I did earlier and him being so stubborn minded, I doubt my efforts will end up yielding any decent result."

"That's fine. Hopefully it's unrelated." Haise continued towards the door, trying not to think about what he'd done, but Lewis held his hand up to stop him.

"You might want to brace yourself . . ." Lewis became more serious, his manner shifting sharply and suddenly.

"For what?" Haise followed him inside and up to their room. They were met by the stern face of Zanita and a much-paler Maple, as though she had been in a baking mishap and flour were the antagonist.

"Care to explain what you lot have been doin' in my inn?" Zanita snarled.

Haise looked at Lewis's remorseful eyes and back to Maple. Taking in the room, he felt his face slowly drain of colour as it dawned on him. *They found out! How did they find out?*

Haise thought back on the illusion he had cast; the items had been simple, uninteresting. Perhaps Maple had been curious about one of the books or moved the vase, revealing the sliced eye and its putrid contents. Maybe Zanita had opened the door for whatever reason and, with sheer muscular force, knocked something off the table.

His mind was racing with what to say, how to explain this, wondering how this had happened in the first place. That's when it struck him.

He had failed to remember one flaw in the illusion incantation: The caster had to remain within a certain radius of the illusion or it would fall. He'd gone too far into the forest searching for the woodsman, and it had broken. *Damn it.*

He had done quite a foolish thing. To make matters worse, he still had no idea what they were dealing with. Inaction and action were both powerful forces and, in this case, both detrimental. He was torn between apologising for what he'd done and acknowledging that it had to be done whether they liked it or not.

People desired an explanation for things they didn't understand, and if one wasn't given, it fell to the folly of the mind to provide it, so reason would slip and allow insanity to take its place. He needed an answer, one that would regain him and Lewis at least a small portion of trust.

"They're a demonic entity residing in the worlds of both flora and fauna, called the Bones of Passion. It weaves its way through the entire body, entwining the victims' bones in a passionate embrace of death. That is what you face, what you will all face if I don't find a cure."

The room fell silent. No one moved or talked for what seemed like an eternity. Stress gripped Haise's insides, and voices whispered of passing time as anxiety ran rampant in his heart.

"We don't have time for this," Haise blurted. He felt the weight of the tragedy stronger than he'd ever thought he would. He was so tired, so exhausted. "The mortality of this situation should be obvious by now!"

Lewis placed a hand on Haise's shoulder. Haise took a moment to breathe before he continued, "Samuel is dead. Benny is likely to die soon, and if I ever hope to find a solution, I need to study this plant. It's completely sealed and safe, but I understand it's intimidating. I need your trust for a little longer. I promise an antidote is close at hand."

At this, Zanita's cold expression weakened, and Maple covered her mouth, her eyes brimming with tears. He needed to see Benny. If what had happened to Samuel was developing inside Benny, he had little time. Haise knew saving him was impossible at this point, but he could at least bring the family and friends together for Benny's sake.

"If I'm to save anyone from this, save them from their fate, I need time, a place to study," Haise pleaded, hoping to appeal to their better nature.

"If it is as you say, then stay. But ya better find a way to help these people. They don't deserve a fate like this," Zanita grumbled as she gripped Maple's shoulder and turned. "We're goin'. Follow if ya want."

Haise's resolve crumpled, his composure deteriorating as they disappeared through the door. Lewis leaned towards him and tried to lift his mood. "Nice save, but now we definitely can't skip town if this doesn't work out."

Haise raised a brow. "As if we ever would."

"Also, the Bones of Passion?" Lewis repeated, his brow quirking.

"Passion as in the fruit, the plant . . . and since it's made of bones and flesh . . . well, it seemed good at the time, okay?" Haise pouted.

Lewis chuckled. "Oh no. No, it's great."

Haise's face was deadpan. In all seriousness, he shouldn't be smiling right now, but he was so grateful Lewis was here.

"Come on, we should follow," Haise said, pulling a brave face again and steeling himself for what was to come.

# Chapter 24

The air in Benny's home was thicker than ever, and Haise's pomander did very little to alleviate the smell that whispered like words behind backs. The atmosphere felt as though it were born from the thoughts that hung heavy on the mind and soul, transforming into rot that clung to and slipped down the walls.

In the boy's room stood Lin, Michael, Zanita, Maple, and a few others Haise had yet to meet. They mumbled prayers of hope and wishes for his good health to return. Someone had placed a few pillows behind Benny to prop him up, and his eyes were more open than the first time Haise had seen him.

Michael asked Haise, "We heard from Zanita what befell poor Samuel, and now what is happening to Benny. So, there is nothing we can do? Nothing we ever could have done?" It felt rhetorical, causing the question to burn through Haise all the more.

Lewis had warned him. Told him that if he were to help, he could make things worse. Had he done that? Done what he had hoped never to do?

Haise couldn't respond. How did one begin to answer for the things they couldn't control? The more he thought, the stronger those invisible chains tightened around his chest.

Haise was disheartened, and that expression was all Michael needed to understand their predicament.

"I made your favourite sweet pastry." Maple's voice crumbled as she produced one warm, steamy cinnamon scroll. Haise recalled the same smell of spices from the sweet scroll she had given him the first day. Maple had been making Benny's favourite pastry since he and Lewis arrived, perhaps even long before.

Benny tried to thank her, but only his lips moved in response to his command. Lin held his hand from beside the bed on the side opposite Maple, whose eyes were puffy and red from hours of crying. On the other hand, Lin's face was pale and revealed a weighted mind drowning under layers of pain.

Haise felt responsible. He should have been faster. Should have done better.

The worst part was yet to come. Soon, the vines would burst through the skin, and Benny's body would twist, morphing to serve their wicked whims. He would attack his parents and his friends. Everyone, no matter how dear to him in life, would become nothing to him in death. Haise had to do something before that happened.

He saw Lin raise her hand towards him. She had been studying his face as he had studied hers. She would have noticed his hesitation, his anxious glances. Placing his hand in hers, she gently pulled him closer and lowered his hand to Benny's chest. It was like she knew. Knew what Haise had to do.

He couldn't use his instrument here with all the other people present. They would die if they heard "Song of Rest" unless they were as powerful as or stronger than he was, like Lewis.

The silence between Haise and Lin was incredibly loud, yet only Lewis heard the ruckus. He placed a hand on Haise's shoulder, and a slight nod of understanding followed his warm and solemn smile. Haise felt more assured that what he had decided to do was for the best. *This is right . . .*

He focused his mind on the point of contact and released his qi into Benny's bloodstream. He had one more option available if music couldn't be used. By gently manipulating his qi flow to fluctuate in strength, he could cause vibrations.

The more concentrated it was, the higher the pitch, and vice versa. He'd found out he could do this long ago when humming to his mother. Like Haise, she would get sick a lot, but his humming seemed to help ease her discomfort. As a child, he hadn't realised he was using a talent. It wasn't until Hiro spoke about it that Haise had come to know his gift.

"Song of Rest" hummed through his veins, and a tear trickled down Benny's face. It snaked through the growing curves of a smile, an expression that spoke many volumes, a wordless tome of tribute to feelings of fear, acknowledgement, and peace. A quietness befell his face, one of rest rather than pain, even as those surrounding him were felled by the weight of overwhelming grief.

Haise left his qi to gently flow like blood through the boy, mimicking life and buying the family enough time to cremate Benny's body. He quietly slipped out, letting the broken family mourn; leaving, too, some shattered part of himself behind. Lewis's voice reached out to him, but there was no room for his kindness within the chaos of Haise's mind.

A hand on his shoulder had Haise spinning on a dime, his fan blades just hairbreadths from Lewis's throat. Haise paled. His immediate shock reaction was met with a small smile as Lewis gently moved the blades away.

"You did what you had to do, and no one could have done better than you." Lewis's voice eased his rampaging heart. Haise slumped over, his head resting against Lewis's chest.

"This was my doing," Haise whispered as his vision blurred. *This is all my fault . . .*

Chapter 25

Back straight, eyes forwards, Haise composed himself amongst the small group gathered near the inn. Lewis immediately went to work easing their minds and setting up the supplies offered by Lord Perch. There were a few large tents, a couple of tables, and, although not many, some futons and tatami mats. Chairs had also been brought out, though Haise wasn't sure by whom.

To Haise's relief, the community had come together after all. Their camaraderie was similar to that of a colony of bees. If only the House of Nyal could show the same degree of interest in their well-being, then perhaps spirits would be higher. At least this time, clan members were tending to the people. Haise noticed that most of them were ill as well.

"I will leave the rest to them and revisit Lord Perch. This time I'll see what I can do about finding information on the strange guy in the alleyway." Lewis spoke quietly so the clan members couldn't accidentally overhear their conversation.

"Don't take any unnecessary risks, okay? Whatever's going on between those two may have nothing to do with this disease."

"Or it could have everything to do with it, but yes. I half promise I won't do anything stupid."

At that, he took off, leaving no time for Haise to pin him down with admonishment. Haise couldn't help but sigh. If it were him doing whatever Lewis was doing, the outcome would be the polar opposite, even if he took the same risks. Haise honestly believed he was cursed to a degree.

He slipped back into the inn and returned to room 202. Upon the table sat, clear as day, the bones and flesh of the parasitic plant. He detested this being and its superior ability to kill, but he knew there must be some weakness, at least one flaw. Nothing in this world was perfect.

"No one at all," he whispered to himself.

He leaned over, grabbed the satchel he had tucked away, and began pulling out his stored herbs. Sewn with qi-infused cotton and embellished with sigils, this handmade satchel could hold far more inside than it would seem. All the herbs and tools for the medicine he had made so far came from this bag.

His supply had dwindled considerably after treating all the people who had gathered earlier, so he set about making more.

If it hadn't been for Lewis coming in much later as the sun's light dwindled, Haise would have run out of herbs. He had become so engrossed that his mind had wandered, and he'd made too much. However, given the circumstances, maybe it wasn't enough.

"Haise, you should get some rest. Transfer the sealing spell to me." Lewis approached his weary friend.

"These are for those with rashes. Give this to anyone with headaches, fevers, coughing, and—"

"Haise."

"These are for those with trouble sleeping, and—"

"Haise, please."

He paused, knowing Lewis could tell he wasn't himself, but there were more important things than a personality shift to be worried about. He was just tired, that was all.

"I'll think about it, but first, what did you learn from the lord?"

Lewis frowned at his redirection but answered anyway. "Daddy made a deal with the devil. Perch has done shady business and formed a blood contract with Liez. I don't know the name, but they're likely a denizen of the demonic realm. It turns out Malachy Perch has more than one child. He also has a daughter, and she became terribly ill, which is why he made a deal with Liez.

"In exchange for Liez cleansing her blood and body of disease, he would surrender his life in place of hers. She was too young to fight this, and Liez agreed. However, he didn't take Perch's life straightaway; otherwise, he wouldn't be here. So, why? It's as though he had a reason not to, or knew something bad would happen soon."

"You think Liez knew of the Bones of Passion before it became the source of this epidemic?" Haise was amazed that Lewis had been able to retrieve this much information by coercing Perch's thought patterns.

"It's not off the table. Perch blamed Liez, believing he was the cause of his daughter getting sick a second time. So, like a moron, he called him out and demanded he actually do what he said he could. Liez came upon request, but Perch had already dug his grave.

"Liez refused to save her from the Bones of Passion, since there was nothing more he could recieve from the lord. Perch then offered his wife's life as well as his. Still, Liez refused. He was no longer interested and left, but I don't know why."

Haise thought about the strangeness of it all. When had Perch gotten in contact with a denizen of the demon realm—and more to the point, how? "Knowing something would happen isn't proof of causing it. Do you think Liez would talk to me?"

Haise watched his friend's face grow dark. "No. You need to be careful, Haise. Liez is a dangerous individual. Don't ever approach him. If he comes to you, run. Create as much distance as you can."

Lewis was serious, so Haise took his words to heart. There was no reason to refute his concerns as paranoia or overexaggeration; Lewis had never once misled him.

"I couldn't distinguish what was so terrifying about him from Perch's thoughts, but something is wrong with him," Lewis continued. Leaving no time for Haise to answer, he quickly shifted to their previous conversation. "I promised I'd help you, and I will in any way you need, so I'll hand these out. But please, transfer that illusion spell to me when I get back." His topic shift tore Haise's mind off the possible danger lurking around town, and although he appreciated the offer, he didn't respond.

He had made his peace with the demands of his current task already and wouldn't place the burden on another. If it became so bad that he could not maintain the spell, he would compromise the specimens from Samuel and seal them in wax. *It's fine. I'm fine . . .*

Lewis quietly left, but no sooner than he had, he returned.

"Haise, we have a problem." Lewis spoke urgently. "I just got word that three more people have died. Their corpses are rampaging through houses."

The disease was giving them no breathing room, as if it knew a cure was nigh. It took Haise a moment to process what he was hearing. He had already seen so many people when the man lost his life in the streets, and those he had treated had told him their family members were doing all right. None had been displaying any symptoms so progressed that it would put anyone at such an immediate risk. How had he let this happen? He should have gone door-to-door.

Benny's case had revealed that the illness, though deadly, developed at a steady pace. If Benny's symptoms were similar to those of the individuals Haise had treated recently, they should still be alive and continue to be so for at least another week. He had relied too heavily on the people to spread word of the medicine available at the inn and missed too many who had been struck ill.

A whispering voice tightened his chest. It spoke of ruin caused by gods who mingled with mortals. A part of him resisted the idea, a part believed it was true, and another part was silent.

Haise's thoughts moved to Samuel. He had died but, unlike the others, had not run amok. The difference occurred to him. Samuel had been missing an essential part of his body. Perhaps the demonic plant needed the epicentre. It must use the mind and its vine tendrils to control the body.

"Decapitation," Haise murmured.

"What?"

"The only way to quickly stop them without causing damage by using fire is . . . decapitation." Haise moved to get up, and Lewis sat him back down.

"Rest. I'll deal with this." Before Haise could protest, Lewis was gone. The sun was retiring, the room felt cold, and

Haise didn't want to spend another moment in front of segmented bone and crushed eye pollen.

Leaving everything where it was, he went to each room to check on the isolated patients and ensure they were okay and that nothing new was ailing them. Apart from being a bit thirsty, all of them were stable.

Outside appeared to be a different story. Underneath one of the tents Lewis had helped put up earlier was a man who had begun yelling at one of the clan officials. From the window, Haise could just make out that he was gripping the front of the official's shirt. The clan member was trying their best to calm the man down.

Haise raced downstairs and out the front. "Everything okay? Is there something I can help you with, sir?" Haise took a gentle approach. He preferred understanding each person's issue and position before assuming his own. The man might have reason to yell, or he might not. If there was to be a quick and straightforward solution, one must never jump to conclusions.

"This man is refusing to give me more medicine! I'm still sick, and so is my family! I demand you give me more! I know the lord has his own source of medicine, but that guy is only helping him. Why? What about us? He should be helping his people, not just his own."

So even citizens had seen the lord and the tall man together. Their seemingly private meetings in alleyways were not so secret after all. Haise slowly approached, but just as he came within a few feet, the man lunged, but not at Haise. He redirected his anger back onto the official, completely ignoring Haise.

Haise didn't know whether to be shocked or confused. He had known the man would lose his cool, but he had never expected this reaction. The man turned with such speed that Haise had only moments to intervene before anyone got hurt.

Haise could separate them with a few well-placed taps and pushes, but after such little sleep, he saw double. He blinked a few times. Still two. Sleep deprivation was a scary thing. How long had it been since he'd slept? One, two, perhaps three days. He was losing count of the hours. *I could have leant on Lewis, but . . .*

The man was not so easily silenced, and as his hand reached out, Haise tried to defend himself. He went to grab the incoming hand and missed. A fist grabbed his shirt, lifted him, and threw him. The ground reached out and stole his voice, his air, his sight. Stars twinkled in his darkened world, and his already-weakened body fell deeper into the gloom under the weight of mistreatment.

He rolled to right himself, but all these lives upon his shoulders were more than a great burden: They were punishment. The sense sealing broke as Haise got to his feet, and the eyes he'd taken from the flowers sprouting out of

Samuel tumbled from his pouch, bursting on impact with the ground. Spores flowed out.

They first burrowed into the man's skin, then the official's, then encroached on those around them. Screams sowed waves of dread through the crowd as groans and gurgling noises pushed their way through the throats of the deceased. The man and the official died immediately, flowers blooming from their chests and heads. Blood trickled down, twisting faces as unfurling petals pushed through mouths and eyes.

Haise trembled as he pushed off his knees. Each second it took him to recover was another second the infection spread. Thanks to Lewis, all of those who had gathered to receive medicinal herbs had already left. Those who'd remained were likely relatives of the isolated, present under false pretences, or here with motives similar to the man who had addressed the official. They were now running for their lives or paralysed with fear.

Simply putting distance between them and this tent would hold no saving grace. They were too close initially, and all Haise could do was watch as they stumbled, fell, and reanimated. He returned his attention to the closest pair as they both aimed their malice towards him. Haise retreated from grabbing hands, only to notice the runners making a speedy return.

His fingers brushed his lyre. None but the dead were close enough to be affected by his song. They staggered closer, their breath hot with decay.

This called for a last resort.

 # Chapter 26

Sharp strings hummed under Haise's touch. Flowing notes poured like mellow red wine from Akin as though they found glee in the whispered words of death. The rhythmic lilt brought woe to most who heard its plea. Those strong enough to resist would still drown in sorrow and misfortune.

This was only the second time Haise had played this song. The other had been whilst it was being created. The man who had started the uproar came in and out of focus as Haise concentrated on his notes.

A flicker of movement had his head tilting and his fingers hesitating. It was Lewis.

Why is Lewis here? Panic-stricken, Haise almost stopped playing until Lewis flashed by, instantly decapitating the man, who had gotten far too close for comfort.

"Don't stop." Lewis spoke in passing before giving the official equal treatment. Haise prayed the song wouldn't affect him too harshly. Lewis was no doubt stronger than him, but the song could grip anyone.

Still, he was more powerful than most gods Haise knew. As the final note of "Ballad of Death" took flight, the dead froze. The song was more than a melody of demise. It had never been designed to specifically attack anything during its creation. Instead, it homed in on qi, the life force and power of all things, and obliterated it within a small area around the caster. That was why individuals with incredible strength still found it hard to withstand the draining effects of the sound.

The Bones of Passion stood no chance against its merciless assault, so the battle was over within moments. Each victim crumpled as though they had all succumbed to sleep. Haise wobbled on his feet, the song having drawn out what little qi he had left. Eyes drooping, he stepped back, trying to compose himself, only to find Lewis standing right behind him. Lewis supported him, allowing him a much-needed respite.

"Thank you," Haise mumbled. *Well, I'm leaning on him now . . .*

Haise scoffed at himself. He had been far too consumed by his desire to help that his actions had become unguided, causing more harm than good. Why had he thought he could help these people with no repercussions?

"Don't mention it." Lewis moved to hold him better and said, "Incendium." All the bodies caught fire, and ash drifted up like black snow.

Haise's teeth clenched as he bit back the urge to cry. This pain was strikingly deep and vicious, but it was nothing compared to the turmoil he had felt back then at the festival.

The skies mirrored the flames as the setting sun burned this moment into history. Haise spotted a single spore wafting towards him as he gathered himself. Curiously he watched it as it floated down. He did nothing to halt its path, and it landed on his hand.

Intrusive thoughts told him he deserved as much, but it turned to ash on contact. Haise was positive the spore hadn't been burned by the fire nor damaged in any way. Part of the solution had been staring him down this whole time: his immortality. All immortals were free from illness, and nothing could infect their blood.

Including his blood in the medicine for those who had fallen ill could alter its effects or even multiply its effectiveness, but to what end? It could cure them or kill them. There were reasons no one had noted its effects; it was a great sin to sully the blood of a god for the sake of a mortal.

Was this another foolish hope, like the ghost who had yet to show herself again? There were some ways to discover its effects, but the fastest would be to give it to one of the isolated.

Haise wondered where the line between right and wrong rested. Whether at any point he had crossed that line. Was the world ever black and white to begin with? No, such a boundary would never exist, lest it make decisions far too simplistic and the consequences more predictable. With excellent contrast came clarity of mind; such a contrast had completely escaped Haise's reality.

But this would not halt his actions, even as he broke his promise to Lewis, who had reminded him that he shouldn't have come this far. Although Haise didn't want to believe his presence had caused more harm, there was little to refute the point.

With Lewis's quiet support, Haise returned to their room in the inn. He made the new medicine, then left the room again to randomly select an isolated individual. All these patients had slipped into unconsciousness, and with no time to obtain permission from a family member, Haise had no choice but to take the blame if anything were to happen.

"Are you sure about this? There are no viable records for how immortal blood can affect the mortal body." Lewis's concern touched Haise, but it wasn't enough to sow a seed of doubt and halt his hand.

"Time will tell its tale, so best we wait and listen."

"Then you have time to rest now, so please do. I can watch over them and see if your blood makes a difference."

Haise hesitated. He was desperately tired . . . so what stopped him from listening to Lewis? He felt like he was missing yet another blatant truth, one that itched at his conscience. It was tantalisingly close but just out of reach, providing mere glimpses of an idea, like when one saw a subtle movement out of the corner of one's eye.

"What happened to that ghost?"

"I haven't seen it or heard anything about it recently. Why?"

"It's just strange, don't you think? It shows up around the same time this illness does but disappears before it's lifted. It's as though it was simply a coincidence," Haise said as he returned to the corridor, looking down at the inn tables below, the balustrade the only thing separating him from the first floor.

"You don't think that, though, do you?"

"Mmm." Haise felt positive the two events were somehow connected; as to how or why, that would have to wait until the ghost showed herself again.

"I'll retire to our room." Haise walked a few paces and had opened the door to 202 when he heard Maple and Zanita returning. They had most likely joined Benny's family in cremating Benny and celebrating his life. A life much too short.

"What happened?" Zanita yelled. Maple was coughing and shaking from the shock. Her gait was unbalanced, and she looked quite pale. Haise rushed downstairs, slipping past the angry Zanita, and caught Maple before she hit the floor. Her disposition must be weak. Perhaps Haise was no better, not that it would ever stop him from trying to help.

"Please, give me a moment to explain." He lowered her to the floor, supporting her head. Maple remained beautiful, and her purity and kindness had never bowed to prejudice. Her scales had never seemed to mar her character but instead formed a type of armour.

"You're testing my patience, boy. Explaining can only get ya so far." Zanita's arms were crossed, affirming her unyielding personality. Haise knew telling her what had happened wouldn't help. At worst, it could get them evicted. He was so close to a possible cure, so getting kicked out now would be devastating. More than that, it could very well be the end of this town and all the surrounding villages. *Think, think . . .*

"He's awake!" Lewis shouted from the second story. "He just woke up, and almost all his symptoms are gone!"

Lewis always seemed to have perfect timing.

Chapter 27

Haise touched the back of his hand to the man's forehead. "What's your name, and how are you feeling?"

"I'm Davis Curt, and I feel almost as great as I did before my illness. What did you give me? Can you give my family the same? I'm so worried about them. Can I see them now? Are they here?"

"Please be patient. I need to make sure of a few things first, and then you may see your family. Is that all right with you?" Haise spoke earnestly, knowing the man's ordeal could be far from over. He saw a point in false hope, but only to the extent that it wouldn't negatively impact the person should the worst come to fruition.

"Yes. Yes, of . . . of course." Haise noted that Davis still sounded hoarse and the rashes remained. His blood had somehow calmed the body's reactions but done nothing in the way of repair. It was as though the spread has been paused, but for how long remained a mystery.

"Are you still itchy?"

"No. Not really."

"Do you still have a sore throat?"

"Well, it doesn't feel any better." Holding his arms around his chest, the man coughed, wincing at the pain it caused him.

Haise recalled Benny's initial condition when he'd used his ring to determine the state of his body and soul. It was the lungs that had been affected the worst. The most common symptoms were so basic that they matched those of a cold, so he had focused on the rashes, the mass deterioration of system functions, and the terribly high fever that would cause even more problems if not immediately addressed.

Haise pondered the sore throat, the coughing, the lungs, and the spores that had started this all. He considered how the disease was spreading, but not in terms of treatment—only as a preventative measure so he could somewhat contain the number of infected.

"Haise, there seems to be more smoke." Lewis's words drew Haise's gaze to the window and towards thick smoke in the distance lit by the flames of a roaring fire. It was too great to be a cremation, too small to be a wildfire. Lewis took the lead as they left the room through the window and leapt onto the roof of a neighbouring building. From there they could see the blaze and the inky shadows of those who watched the temple burn.

Most of the temple was made of stone, but decorative carvings and its framework became fodder for the flames.

Although the small temple was closer to the forest near the entrance to the town, it was still a far enough distance from the trees that Haise wasn't too worried.

"How could they do this? You were the only one who stayed to help. Ungrateful little . . ." Lewis bent forwards as though to speed off and do god knew what in the name of justice, or perhaps some form of self-gratification. Haise was upset, but the part of him that would protest this, the part that would let Lewis go, had disappeared a long time ago with Yasu.

"Let it burn. It's not important," Haise murmured as he watched flames curl out from and around the temple. Everything barring the stone would no doubt be reduced to ash, and with it, he hoped, so would his honour. That way people would have their villain. In a sea of despair, faith wasn't the only thing that brought people together. It could just as easily be a common enemy.

This meant he would find it difficult, if not impossible, to continue treatment if he couldn't do it right now. His chest felt heavy, and those voices began to plague his thoughts again. He had lost control of the situation. When had he let this go so far?

The fire ebbed from the fallen temple as tears fell from those left behind. Many had died, but none would be forgotten as long as Haise walked this world. He had to find a way to finish what he had started and do it quickly. The heavenly guards would no doubt be watching.

Thinking back to his days in the heavenly realm, he recalled that there had been plenty of new and wondrous things to behold. The contrast between where he had been and where he had lived as a mortal was so great that the golden light had blinded him for a time. In the beginning, it was those things, the splendour of the wealthy, that had captured his attention.

One of the items had been a jade-and-silver incense burner. Its intricate patterns were rendered subpar by three even more impressive dragons. Two formed the handles, and the other curled over the top. Haise burned incense in it every day for months until the glamour of the realm had lost its shimmer.

This thought, plus the smoke that rose from the fire roaring outside, had him immediately leaping back inside to visit the patient who had received his blood . . . and coming face-to-face with Zanita. She must have come into the man's room to keep him company. Her smile dropped to a scowl upon seeing him, and she took a step to put herself between Haise and the man on the bed. Haise could understand her reaction, but it still stung.

"I need to borrow something." He had little energy to muster his composure or be concerned with his appearance. He must do more than persuade her to listen; he must insist he be obeyed. Though he had no chance at intimidation, he knew other, less attractive ways.

Haise pushed his desperation to the surface. This was no time for self-preservation, and he knew all too well how to look as if he were in great need. He wore it for all its worth, as though it were his second skin. She buckled, her brows furrowed, and Haise lunged at the opening she had given.

"I've found a cure, but I'll need an incense burner. Any type will do," he pleaded. Anyone watching him in such a state would have secondhand embarrassment, or even go as far as to mock the gods for his humiliating display. A deity should never beg. A deity should command. Those above might cast condescending glares, Haise thought, but he was not and never would be a god. If he were, none would have perished. What had he been thinking? A foolhearted person could never achieve what they wanted in a situation like this.

"Haise . . ." Lewis was by his side, his tone tentative, and his voice returned Haise to his senses. Tears had run down his cheeks, but when? When had he become so feeble? His determination had dissipated, and in its place hope scrambled for a desired outcome.

Zanita groaned in complaint and left the room, returning with one incense burner. "Here. Do what you came to do, or all those lives will have been lost in vain. Once you're done, you leave."

Lewis went to snarl at her remark, but Haise's soft tug on his coat had him falling back. Instead, Lewis took the incense burner, turning hurt eyes to Haise. Zanita left, and Haise sighed as though he had been holding his breath. The relief made him dizzy.

Haise turned to Davis. "Try to get some rest, and all will be well tomorrow, I'm sure of it." The man lay speechless as they left, only thanking them once they had gone.

. . .

Back in their room, Haise knew he needed to get to work. He didn't know how much time they had, but it wouldn't be much.

"Lewis, place the incense burner on the windowsill and help me prepare these herbs." Haise pulled the last of his medicine and herbs out of his pouch and explained what they had to do. "We're going to mix it with my blood and some crushed pollen, then burn it."

Lewis was stunned by the proposition but did precisely what Haise asked of him.

The incense burner was nothing special; it was simple, plain, and made of white porcelain, with no adornments or etched details. However, it was this simplicity that made it beautiful.

Haise cleaned out the inside, removing anything that might taint the process. As he did that, Lewis ground the pollen with the rest of the dried herbs, adding them to the leftover medicine prepared earlier to treat the cough, sneezing, and sore throat. The other types were put to the side.

Haise rested the incense burner on the windowsill and let Lewis place the herbs in it as though it were a small garden. The smells of flowers and earth were strong yet pleasant. All the while, Haise had been considering the logistics of this endeavour. The *create* spell was incredibly versatile and powerful but could just as easily be weak and lacklustre, depending on the caster's experience. Haise wondered how much oomph was going to be enough. Too weak and his cure wouldn't reach the masses; too strong and he'd risk passing out before it was completed. It was just another fine line he would have to walk.

Adamantly, Lewis said, "No. This time, you will have me. I'm not going anywhere. I refuse to stand by anymore. I know you wanted to be stronger than you were, to do this as best you could alone. But watching you struggle to bear this alone has been torture."

Haise had little effort to protest his help or the fact that he had used his mind influence without consent again.

Protest . . . ? The word made him think. Why did he fight against help? Was it as Lewis said, because he wanted to prove to himself that he could do this and make up for the past?

He had pushed Lewis away, even though he had asked for his help initially. Maybe somewhere deep down, he'd known his efforts would fail and he hadn't wanted to drag Lewis down with him. Perhaps it was more than that, but he wasn't sure anymore.

Haise closed his eyes and stilled his thoughts. For this to work, he needed absolute concentration, which would be difficult. Lewis lit the herbs afire, setting the tiny smouldering leaves curling and shrivelling as though withdrawing from the heat of battle, their victory surrendered to ruin. Wisps of white smoke rose from the aftermath, carrying with them a subtle sweetness and a hint of spice. The woody aroma wrapped around Haise as he conjured images of small rodents, birds, and cats within his mind.

He brushed a finger down one blade of his fan, and drops of crimson began to burn alongside the rest. The metallic note entwined with the smoke, and a sense of heat bloomed around. Quiet power flowed through the current of white, and Lewis readied his blade.

"Scurry, squeeze, and seek. Find all that need your help and relieve them of their blight. Create!" The incense burner grew hotter, and lines of smoke streamed out as if they were being pulled with tremendous force. Hundreds of smoke threads hit the floor and wove small creatures of day and night, their intangible bodies never settling. The roving smoke maintained the shape of the animals as they began to move.

Lewis winced as he ran his blade across his arm. Welling blood surfaced and dripped to the floor. Instantly, the creatures swarmed for a taste, and with that, the creation spell was completed. Once gifted their life and the most crucial part of the medicine, they leapt, hopped, skittered, and flew all over Falk and beyond. Down roads, through houses, over buildings, and across streams, they found those who had left and those who had stayed.

Maple cautiously poked her head into the room, too curious about the strange smoke creatures leaping down the stairs from room 202. Haise turned at the sound of her approach. She was looking at Lewis's arm, which was still bleeding quite fervently.

A small, wispy cat purred as it weaved itself around her legs. Maple's caution morphed into awe as she bent down to pat it. However, the creature had other ideas and moved on. A surprised breath had Maple breathing in some of the smoke, while the remainder wrapped around her as though it were giving her a loving hug.

The spell had worked. Haise knew he shouldn't get too happy because it was still unclear if the medicine worked as well as intended. Maple's smile warmed Haise's heart. He felt a sense of relief for the first time in days. The spell had taken its toll, and he wavered, collapsing into the arms of Lewis, who held him tightly.

His relief was short-lived. The guards of the heavenly realm had come for them both. White light warped the room, and Haise expected to be suddenly pulled into their halls. Instead, every being was still and unmoving.

"Found you, my pitiful creature. To think our king fancies you." The silhouette of a figure bent to one knee, a display that only accentuated their height.

Haise flicked his gaze over the others in the room, including the two guards who had reached through to this realm, their hands already outstretched towards him and Lewis. They seemed unconscious and restricted, their silence suggesting their indisposition. Whoever was orchestrating this takeover had a talent for a rather fascinating method of control.

"We know what your friend can do. Did you think we wouldn't notice him poking around? The taste of Lord Perch's heart is as disgusting as his nature." The figure spoke to Lewis in layered voices, as though more than one person resided in the body. Their white teeth shone as they rose and tilted Lewis's chin. Haise saw that disturbing smile for a second time, and he gasped as the pieces fell into place. The debt had been paid. This was Liez, the tall man from the alleyway. Lewis had said he was bad news, and Haise could tell why.

"Tch." Liez frowned at the guards twitching against his control. "We were too late. Sorry, my king." With that, he was gone, and Falk faded to the light as Haise and Lewis were whisked back to the heavenly realm.

Chapter 28

The quiet dusk of Falk was no more, its stillness broken by the sudden chaos and noise. Haise grimaced at the jostling, his head aching from the onslaught. With so many people speaking at once, it was too hard to tell what was going on.

Wincing at the bright light, he peeked his puffy eyes open. As it all came into focus, Haise's hunch, or rather his foreseen outcome, was coming to pass. They were now facing court in the presence of the Heavenly Emperor.

What he didn't see was any reaction to what had occurred moments before, as if no one had any memory of it. Instead, the glances he was receiving seemed more related to his appearance, which must be beyond dishevelled. Blood from Lewis's arm decorated his back and front, as though he'd come from a massacre or some depraved ritual. At least that idea seemed to be reflected in the many faces staring at him, their eyes piercing holes through his broken armour.

Though it seemed ridiculous to consider, it felt as though he had been set up for failure from the very beginning, but his efforts hadn't been futile. The spell appeared to have been successful, so if it wasn't failure they were after. It was simple: They were after him. It had been a trap from the very beginning.

Haise had known for a while that something immoral was going on amongst a group of gods, unbeknownst to the rest. Not even the Heavenly Emperor gave the impression that he knew, and if he did, he wasn't showing his cards. The more Haise had pried into the matter, the more certain things had felt off, as though he were being watched. His food, home, and medicine were all being tampered with.

A planned exile—that's what was happening. A way to remove him from the equation and the heavenly realm because he was getting too close to a truth some didn't want to surface. In all his nosing around, he had come across only bits and pieces of information that tied the troublemaking gods to the current leader of Dramour, King Emrys. The worst of it was in relation to the calamity-class weapons lost during the Great War.

He was tired, broken, torn, and disappointed in himself, and all the while he'd had to internalise his pain, knowing that if he didn't, that too would be used against him.

This wouldn't last long. The Heavenly Emperor had no choice.

"Haise. Hear me now. You shall walk again amongst the mortal and repent for your actions. You will be stripped of your title and possessions."

"Please. I beg of you. Haise never meant any harm from this. Spear him such harsh judgement!" Lewis begged, mumbling "Please" over and over again. Haise went to reach for him and tell him to stop, but he was quickly and roughly reprimanded by his detainer. With a split lip, he fell silent, choosing instead to yell out in his mind. *Lewis! Stop! Please . . . please. You'll only incur more ire.*

From the corner of his eye, Haise could see Lewis's grimace, as though he were in pain. He had heard. This time, Haise was glad for the intrusion, even more so for his subsequent efforts to soothe Haise's mind.

"Bring me all but the cloth upon his back," the Heavenly Emperor declared, completely ignoring Lewis's plea.

The man standing next to Haise removed his pouches and took his fan. He grabbed Akin, his heavenly weapon, followed by the golden ring. Haise felt more than naked, as though all could see what lay beneath his skin: a mere mortal playing where he shouldn't be, or perhaps worse, a demon or ghost caught trying on masks.

Lewis struggled again, pushing and pulling against not only the guards but also the spell restraints around his wrists and arms. Haise bore the same, though he saw no reason to fight them. For one, he hadn't the energy.

For the briefest of moments, the emperor looked saddened as he pulled Kelheir from its sheath. The holy blade shone brilliantly. Its surface was almost transparent, as though it were light itself. When the edge flicked down, Haise understood that sadness and accepted its meaning. Akin was marred by the weapon, gouged by its heavenly qi.

The name of a weapon gave it incredible power and attached it to its deity. Sometimes a holy weapon could become so linked to its master that name removal not only broke the item but also killed its owner. Haise fell over as his eyes watered, the connections within him dissolving to ash.

The lyre and the fan were the only items returned to him. He stared numbly down at Akin as he ran a finger across the groove, which was still hot from the blade that had taken its power. Coldness flooded his body. He glanced up to see the stern demeanour return to the god of gods.

"May you find peace in your future and wisdom from your past," were the last words the Heavenly Emperor spoke before weightlessness took hold of Haise.

Most of the gods were quiet, but Lewis cried out. His raw scream ripped through the air as Haise slipped between realms. The sound penetrated his soul, tearing open a hole that would never close.

Haise wondered if there was a limit to what people could endure. The coldness spread deeper as Haise said goodbye to another friend. Another person he cherished. Another he would never see again.

He fell to the realm below, the harsh ground his welcoming gift.

. . .

After being cast out, it became almost impossible to live a normal life. He spent what felt like an eternity collapsing over and over, trying to reach somewhere, anywhere, to rest.

A run-down shack flickered through the trees, the sound of footsteps grew louder, and the rippling of fabric whispered in the wind. The figure before him seemed more familiar the closer they got. Their elegance bore witness to a well-educated and refined man. Only one person could ever be so perfect in his eyes.

"Haise . . . ?" His old master, Hiro Foxx, reached out.

When all's said and done, the emperor is a kind person.

Now

Chapter 29

"Haise . . . Haise." Hiro's warm call brought his mind back to the present, to the insane task before them, one he was beginning to consider pointless. He could easily mess this up in the same way or make a wrong decision that would lead them all down the worst path imaginable.

Kuro would find him if he gave up, but the others would be safe. Continuing to cling to life was such a selfish act when others were so ephemeral.

A nose pushed his hand up and through the fur of his demon companion. Wulf was trying to comfort him, even going as far as to wave his tail.

"Ah, Wulf. Thanks." Haise snuggled into his fur. Hiro smiled warmly, as though thanking Wulf for his fluffy assistance.

"One night, and we will leave first thing in the morning." Hiro guided him delicately out of the temple as though he were thin glass about to shatter. Old scorch marks proclaimed the tale of its past, and memories of the bright fire engulfed Haise's view.

He knew he honoured the dead and their families by remembering their plight. Forgetting would be equivalent to dismissing the hell they'd gone through because of him. Still, it had all happened so many years ago that he had hoped those events would cease to control him. He wished that what he'd felt back then would become nothing more than powerless emotions attached to a distant memory.

Vallas looked on questioningly, and Hiro waved her on. "Haise wanted to pay his respects."

"That it? I thought something was up. It's like you saw a ghost." She made a ghoulish face and wiggled her fingers. Haise couldn't help but grin at her dorky expression.

Hiro gave Haise the same questioningly look Vallas had, but Haise paused. He wanted to avoid coming off as rude, since his mood wasn't the best at the moment. Being in restricted quarters might cause him to act in ways or say things he otherwise wouldn't.

"Wulf." Haise ushered him closer and crawled onto his back, pleading quietly that he would allow it. Usually Wulf wouldn't hesitate to throw him off. This time was different. He showed no sign of annoyance and made no move other than to continue forwards, following the cart as it travelled farther into town.

Haise ignored the people who stopped to whisper about the large wolf. Hushed words of amazement and horror were the same no matter where they went. The Clan of Falk's estate loomed ahead. Within its walls were the House of Nyal, the home of Lord Perch and his family, and the aviary. Messenger birds were used throughout the land, and the largest loft was here in Falk, the epicentre of its entire operation.

The guards stepped aside. Delfir must have sent a letter announcing the arrival of Hiro and his party ahead of time. It was customary for cultivators of the spiritual arts to greet the lord or lady of the house when passing through. At times when there was neither, one would acknowledge the presence of whatever higher power served the citizens, hence Hiro's meeting with the priestess in Hamstead and why they were now waiting by the entrance to Lord Perch's ceremonial hall.

"You may enter," the escort declared. Haise reluctantly hopped off Wulf as the beast slipped into the veil. It was better to be safe than sorry. He disliked the idea of his companion being shunned again by people unable to see the wolf for who he was.

With its new alterations, the hall was much grander than it used to be. Opulent chandeliers painted glinting fractures of light over lavish fabrics hung between highly polished marble pillars. Haise could pick out a few things that remained from a period long before this lord's birth.

By this point, the young man walking towards them would likely be Lord Bracken Perch's grandson, which made Haise feel quite old. Many gods were enamoured with their immortal bodies, grateful for the absence of grey hair and aging skin. On the other hand, Haise believed white hair would have suited him. For him, the idea of aging never threw a guise over the beauty time could bestow.

"Lord Foxx! Good to see you. How have you been?"

Hiro had travelled a lot before Haise stumbled back into his life, and Haise wondered if Hiro missed it.

"I am well, Lord Perch. How is your family? The last time I visited, you were soon to be a father," Hiro answered, restricting his conversation to what the moment called for. But Lord Perch had disregarded Haise's and Vallas's presence, and Haise could tell Hiro was vexed.

"Aargh, yes. The child was too sickly and passed. No matter; another can be born. Come, come. I'll get someone to retrieve your letter, so let us drink," Lord Perch said with no display of emotion. Siring an heir was oftentimes seen as a duty, not an intimate moment of connection. Haise understood the notion but despised it and the way those heirs were eventually treated.

Servants hurriedly followed as the lord left the room, motioning the rest to follow. His dismissal of proper etiquette put Haise and Vallas in an uncomfortable position, though Vallas didn't appear to care. Since the lord had not greeted them, they were not permitted to join the conversation as they continued down the corridors, passing various antiques, paintings, and scrolls.

"You have good luck, my friend," Lord Perch continued. "A caravan of wondrous goods is passing through. They have many interesting things. I even commissioned the painter travelling with them to recapture the image of that horrid being."

Hiro faltered at his words. The new painting hanging on the wall depicted a depraved figure with torn clothing, a long nose, a red face, and horns poking through the deep curves of its frown. Haise thought the image was amusing, and how it was captured gave it a sense of life. It appeared silly at surface level. Nonetheless, it was meticulously detailed and hinted at a story beneath the paint.

"Your servants must not know the tale of the mimic and his evil ghost, their trickery beyond wicked!"

Haise had a niggling feeling he wouldn't like where this was heading.

"A fake god conspired with ghosts to inflict Falk with disease and pretend to help to gain new devotees. As if they could make Falk fall. How despicable! Am I right?" His laughter at the prospect was most beastly.

The wall before Haise honoured the dead who'd suffered because a man impersonating a god had caused them much misfortune. It displayed the skewed history of Falk through art and written effigies. Haise felt the sharp sting of remorse as guilt sneered at him from within, yet he smiled. He was grateful that those who had passed were being remembered and now given the respect they had deserved at the time.

Hiro's jaw tensed as he said, "Yes, Lord Perch, though we must not forget that the past can lie as the years go by."

Perch chuckled. "All was good when they both disappeared! My friend, I think age has gotten to you instead."

Vallas's gaze flicked between Hiro and Haise, her expression morphing from boredom to confusion. Hiro was visually torn between his duty to appease the lord and wanting to ensure Haise didn't take the comment to heart.

Unbeknownst to him, Haise was relieved. After he was cast out, the ghost hadn't continued to cause grief to the people. He sighed. Although her appearance was suspicious and they'd never found out why she was there, her disappearance made accepting this new image of himself far easier than it should have been.

Vallas patted him on the back. "This is boring. Never asked for a history lesson, Pops." She chuckled. "It's gettin' late. We're going downtown to the inn. Meetcha there, Hiro."

She grabbed Haise and yanked him off down the hall, away from his troubled master and into Falk's nightlife.

"What was that all about, and why did Hiro look so angry? I've never seen his face look like that. Kinda scary." She rubbed her arms as her wings shivered, her presence causing the flow of people around them to split.

Haise could easily see her beauty, and although she was a descendant of the spirit-kissed, no one looked upon her with judgement. If anything, their glances were sultry. Even the women blushed at her muscular body. *I'm surrounded by beautiful people,* Haise sighed.

"It's a long story." He squinted up to the heavenly realm as though expecting to be blinded by its opulence, but for him, no such castle sat amongst the clouds anymore.

"All I have is time." She peered at him questioningly.

He had no reason to hide the truth from her.

"I was that god."

# Epilogue

Another inn, another night. The trip so far had been less than pleasant, as one thing after another had caused his throat to tighten. Trapped. Haise felt a constant pull, a need to run, but to where, he couldn't say.

At least the only similarity to Hamstead's room was the fireplace. It crackled with heat and spat embers of light as wood settled further into cinders.

The window had been left open during the day, and no one had come to close it. The warmth battled with the cold air and lost before it had even begun, but it was the crane that had his attention.

It took one look at him before leaping off the windowsill, its pure-white feathers too thin to be real. If the creation was here, then was the demon king also watching him? The idea seemed absurd.

Steam rose from a sweet bun and cinnamon scroll on the ledge below the windowsill where the bird had perched, and next to it lay a single flower that matched the ones found in the shrine. The familiar smell of spices grabbed his attention.

"Strange," he mumbled as he grabbed the items and retreated from the cold. "I guess it would be a shame for it to go to waste." Sure, there was a mini him that told him not to, that it was probably laced with poison. But . . . they were sweets. *Mmmm.*

Haise could see his breath as the light faded behind tall evergreen trees. It was getting much colder, the bitterness reminding him of those dazzling festival lights yet again.

The warmth from spices and fresh pastry made the wind less unpleasant and the events of his past more bearable. Lanterns speckled throughout town blurred into stars as though they, too, had fallen with no more wishes left to grant. Drops of rain dappled the paths as grey blotted out the moonlight.

"Why do these memories keep coming back to me?" he mumbled, though the question was stale and moot. This time he had the shrine and the beautiful flower still laced with dew. The sweet bun, the spicy aroma, and the flickering flames. If he had only been stronger those many years ago, he could have saved Yasu and done more for Falk's people.

"If I had just . . ." He trailed off. It was all compiling, his mind crumbling before him, spilling through his fingers. Nothing would make the truth less painful, but he refused to give in, to allow himself to cave to its hand. Haise vowed he would always be waiting, that he would be strong enough in time.

There was a soft brush, a semblance of touch, against his cheek. He heard a gentle humming turn to whispered words from somewhere distant, yet so close he could feel the vibrations. Silver eyes glinted back at him from the partly open window.

"They can't see you how I do." Warm breath touched Haise's ear, and he dropped the flower. He remembered this feeling, recalled the song from the rift and the man who stood within its depths. His velvet voice caused Haise to blush and a strange heat to blossom within him. Were they the same after all?

A hand slipped down his arm and released the bandage's hold. Fabric pooled on the floor, revealing a completely healed wound with only a scar to remind Haise of what had been. A sigh tickled his neck, as though Walker were relieved by what he saw.

"Haise, you're not alone anymore. I won't allow anything else to hurt you again." Walker's voice was rough with anger and filled with desire.

"I was never alone." Haise paused. It was true that he had the others, yet the words were like a lie, ensnaring him within false happiness. No matter who he found himself with, a part of him always felt as though he were alone. Still running, trying to escape the visions of his past.

Walker tilted his head, eyeing him from the glass, as Haise's gaze settled on his own reflection. He disliked what he saw, a reminder of his shamefulness. Walker's brows knitted as if angered by his expression.

"A dear friend of mine from long ago saved me from the depths of my despair." Walker shifted as he spoke, and a small wooden crane painted all white with a circlet on top of its head peeked out from the fabric around his waist. "You don't have to run anymore." Walker spoke softly.

The odd sense of relief that washed over Haise was surprising. With those few words, he felt his legs go weak.

"It's my turn to pay this kindness forwards," Walker continued as Haise tried to process what was happening.

The wooden crane and those gently hummed notes playfully nudged Haise towards the moments he held so dear. Yasu's smile and grimace flickered back and forth in his memory, each fighting to take precedence. It was their song. This was his gift. Hushed thoughts crept forwards, spinning tales of secret unforeseen moments that until now Haise had been blind to. Walker was no stranger.

"How do you know that song?" His eyes blurred with understanding. He knew, yet he couldn't believe it. All this time, Haise had tried so hard to reach him, refusing to accept that Yasu had died. Nothing had ever come of his desperate pleas, no matter how much he'd asked himself and others, "Where is Yasu?" "Is he okay?" "Do you remember me?"

The void within him ached as silent tears slipped from their cage, and with chaos shredding his thoughts, his broken voice barked, "Yasu . . . you jerk!"

The words didn't faze his friend, but a coldness shifted into place.

"I'm sorry, Haise."

There was a pause. A moment of hesitation.

"It seeks your death . . . because of me."

Thank you for reading!

Catch my updates on:

Instagram: @nemu_sai

Tik Tok: @nemu_sai

Cara: @nemusai